Dr Tony Larsen might be a competent doctor, but he badly needed a lesson in professional behaviour, and it suddenly occurred to Sam that she was in the perfect position to administer that lesson.

As he finished testing what she knew to be her cranial nerves, she asked naïvely, 'Do you think I'm going to be all right, Doctor?'

'Oh, yes!' he said, continuing with his examination and not so much as looking at her.

'So the trigeminal nerve is intact, Doctor?'

His head jerked round and he stared at her silently for a long moment. She met his gaze and saw comprehension dawning on his face.

The little minx. She'd been sending him up!

For Judith Hunte, writing medical romances is a happy merging of two major interests, nursing and writing. Judith worked for several years as a librarian before beginning nursing training, eventually qualifying as a registered nurse and midwife. She left nursing to marry and have her family, a son and two daughters, then returned to work in various Australian hospitals for several years.

Early retirement has given her the opportunity to indulge a lifelong yen to write. Her own nursing experience provides the background for her stories.

Previous Titles

ENTER DOCTOR JONES
LOVE AND DOCTOR ADAMS

THE KEY TO DR LARSEN

BY

JUDITH HUNTE

MILLS & BOON LIMITED
ETON HOUSE   18–24 PARADISE ROAD
RICHMOND   SURREY   TW9 1SR

First published in Great Britain 1992
by Mills & Boon Limited

© Judith Hunte 1992

Australian copyright 1992
Philippine copyright 1992
This edition 1992

ISBN 0 263 77525 9

Set in 10 on 11 pt Linotron Baskerville
03-9201-57857
Typeset in Great Britain by Centracet, Cambridge
Made and printed in Great Britain

CHAPTER ONE

CONSCIOUSNESS returned slowly.

It was as though she was pulling herself up from the depths of a murky pond by whatever frail handhold she could find. There were voices, purposeful, intent. And footsteps, rubber soles, squeaking slightly on a polished floor. Then the sound of a trolley, being wheeled quickly.

Even before she could summon the strength to open her eyes or distinguish what the voices were saying, she knew that she was in a hospital ward, and that it was a ward under pressure of an emergency of some kind.

Her instinct told her she shouldn't be lying here. She should be responding to the crisis. She moved her head restlessly on the pillow, but a sharp pain stabbed behind her eyes and she groaned softly.

Immediately, footsteps moved across the floor and stopped beside her bed. Cool fingers grasped her wrist and a female voice asked, 'Are you awake, lass?'

She began to nod, but the pain jabbed again and, instead, she murmured something incoherently and managed to open her eyes. A kind, round, middle-aged face framed in greying hair floated above her.

'How do you feel?'

'My head aches.'

'I'm not surprised. Doctor will be in to see you soon and decide whether you can have something for the pain.'

Samantha murmured something intended to convey understanding. If she had concussion, and it was pretty obvious she had, analgesics were certainly not indicated.

'In the meantime, why don't you go back to sleep?'

'I'll try.'

Sister moved quickly back across the room, pushing through the curtains around the bed opposite Samantha's. As the curtains parted briefly, Samantha glimpsed the occupant of the bed—a young girl of fifteen or sixteen, with brown curly hair. A doctor in a white coat was leaning over her. Here, clearly, was the emergency Samantha had sensed in her semi-conscious state. Again she felt frustrated, angry, that she wasn't able to do anything. She raised her head, then dropped it quickly as the room spun sickeningly.

Sister was right: sleep was her best option in the circumstances. She closed her eyes.

Next time it was a more gentle awakening, as if from natural sleep. Even so, it was some seconds before she felt inclined to open her eyes, and during that time she was aware that someone was standing beside her bed. She stirred, and this time it was a man's voice that asked, 'Are you awake?'

She opened her eyes, then opened them wider still, trying to bring into focus the face floating above her. As her vision cleared, she found she was looking into dark brown eyes, set in a tanned, strong, Aussie sort of face that seemed a little out of place above a white coat and dangling stethoscope.

Whatever! He was a doctor, and a doctor seemed to be her need of the moment. Though he was being rather slow responding to her return to consciousness. . .

Dr Tony Larsen was aware of that, and more. The fact was, he had been standing like a stunned mullet, gazing down at the sleeping patient, for several seconds longer than was necessary to assess her degree of pallor and the depth and regularity of her breathing.

What was more, now that she was awake, he was finding it extraordinarily difficult to concentrate on the size of her pupils, rather than on the colour of her eyes—

a deep azure blue, framed and enhanced by long black lashes.

It was a good thing Sister Benson wasn't in attendance on the other side of the bed; she was a canny old soul, and his momentary loss of professional objectivity wouldn't have gone unnoticed.

His silence lasted so long that Samantha realised she was going to have to take the initiative.

'Hello,' she said tentatively.

'Good morning,' he responded somewhat stiffly. 'Do you know where you are?'

She smiled, a small rueful smile that caused a dimple to dance momentarily beside her lips.

'At a guess, I'd say I'm in a hospital, somewhere east of the Nullarbor Desert. And feeling rather groggy.'

She had an accent. English. Of course, thought Tony—that accounted for the flawless complexion. Though lightly, evenly tanned, her skin had clearly never suffered the ravages of summers spent in the Australian sun.

She was looking up at him, again waiting for him to speak. Feeling, for some reason, compelled to establish firmly who was in control of this consultation, he removed a black fountain pen from his top pocket and flipped through the pages of her case-notes. There were details of her condition on admission and observations that had been charted since, but nothing at all of a personal nature.

'We don't seem to have your name,' he said, and was aware that his voice was unusually brusque.

'It's Sam—for Samantha. Samantha Hayes.'

He wrote on the chart.

'Age?'

'Twenty-three.'

'Home address?'

'My home's in London. Do you want——?'

'Doctor, could I interrupt?'

The middle-aged sister whom Sam had seen earlier was standing behind the doctor. He put Sam's case-notes on her locker and moved to the end of the bed.

'Certainly, Joan. What's the problem?'

'The patient in Room Four has become very restless since you saw him.'

'Then we'd better go ahead with the sedation we discussed. Here, I'll sign for it.' He took the chart Sister held out to him and scrawled quickly on it.

It was all very routine. What intrigued Sam, as she lay watching, was the change in the doctor's manner. As soon as he had begun talking to Sister, he had dropped the stiff formality with which he had been speaking to Sam and had become relaxed, cordial, friendly.

She knew she could be over-sensitive because of the way she was feeling. Her head was pounding heavily and she was increasingly aware of aches and pains in every part of her body. What she really needed was a little tender loving care—that TLC that was supposed to be the hallmark of the medical profession, and which she was more used to giving than receiving. But this doctor seemed never to have heard of it.

Frankly, she thought his bedside manner appalling. So much so, in fact, that she couldn't help wondering whether he had, for some reason, taken an instant dislike to her. She stirred restlessly, and Sister moved up to stand beside her, patting her hand.

'Are you feeling better now, lass?' she asked, with the sympathy Sam had been longing for. Maddeningly, it brought tears to her eyes, and she could only nod mutely. Sister patted her hand again. 'Give it time, lass, give it time.' Then, clearly in a hurry, she took her chart from the doctor, saying, 'Thanks, Tony. Ring if you need a nurse,' and bustled out.

'Well now! Have you any recollection of the accident?'

The cold formality was back. He sounds quite bored with the whole business, Sam thought indignantly. But she answered as best she could.

'I remember up to a point.'

'Up to which point?'

'The point at which I passed out, I presume,' she said, not caring that her irritation showed.

'Mmm. Fair enough.'

He pulled the stethoscope from his neck and began to check her blood pressure, using the sphygmomanometer at the bedhead. He grunted, apparently satisfied, then picked up an ophthalmoscope from a trolley behind him and lowered his face to hers, shining the light into one eye, then the other.

The examination proceeded. And the questions. Sam replied, 'No.' 'Yes.' 'I think so.' 'A little.' And occasionally, 'Ouch!' as his probing fingers found a tender spot.

She was intrigued. The man might look as though he would be more at ease on a horse's back than beside a hospital bed, but he certainly was no slouch as a doctor. In fact, Sam realised before long that she was being given as thorough a neurological assessment as it had been her privilege to witness in four years of training.

And really, she thought, watching him covertly as he worked, his looks, in that rugged, outdoor sort of fashion, were as impressive as his work. His tanned face had paler creases at the corners of his eyes and vertical lines either side of his mouth, lines which became more pronounced when he concentrated. She imagined they became even deeper when he smiled—if he ever did. His hair was thick and dark with just a few grey hairs at the temples.

He seemed unaware of her scrutiny. In fact, he seemed unaware of *her*, except as a collection of bones and muscles, ligaments and nerves. She automatically did what she was told—raising this, tensing that, turning here, looking there, but feeling less and less like a human being and more and more like a 'case'. She thought resentfully that she might just as well have been the demo doll in a lecture-room for all the interest he was showing in her as a person.

She realised he had had to repeat his last question. 'I'm sorry. What did you say?'

'I asked did you know you have stitches in your leg?'

'No, I didn't know that. Did you put them in?'

'No, my colleague did. I was tied up elsewhere at the time. Now, move your toes. . .'

Really! thought Sam. Doesn't it occur to him that I might just happen to be interested in the extent of the injury to my leg—how many stitches there are. . .?

He might be a competent doctor, but he badly needed a lesson in professional behaviour. It occurred to her suddenly that she was in the perfect position to administer that lesson, and could barely repress a smile as she contemplated the form it would take.

As he finished testing what she knew to be her cranial nerves, she asked naïvely, 'Do you think I'm going to be all right, Doctor?'

'Oh, yes!' he said, continuing with his examination and not so much as looking at her. 'You needn't worry—these tests are just routine. We have to make sure you haven't done yourself any damage on the inside.'

'I see. Thank you for explaining,' she said meekly.

'Now, close your eyes tightly and tell me whether you can feel anything touching your face.'

She closed them obediently and said, 'Yes,' 'Yes,' 'Yes,' and 'Yes,' as he touched her forehead, cheeks and mouth with a wisp of cottonwool.

'That's fine. Open your eyes now.'

She did so, then asked in the same meek tone of voice, 'So the trigeminal nerve is intact, Doctor?'

At least her question had the effect of making him

look at her. His head jerked round and he stared at her silently for a long moment. She met his gaze challengingly and saw comprehension dawning on his face.

The little minx. She'd been sending him up!

His hands itched to turn her over and administer some very unprofessional punishment to a certain portion of her anatomy. But his own reaction to the sudden clear anatomical picture that flashed into his mind convinced him that the wisest course of action would be to finish up and get out of here—pronto!

When he could trust himself to speak, he said icily, 'I take it you're either a nurse or a doctor?'

'Oh, not a doctor—just a nurse!'

The words might have been self-deprecating, but the look in her eyes was anything but.

He replied with heavy sarcasm, 'I seem to have been wasting my time doing a neurological examination on you. Clearly you have all your wits about you.'

'My head feels much better, thank you. But mightn't there still be some damage on the. . .inside. . .?' Her voice trailed away before the flush of anger that darkened his cheeks.

'And there might be some other patients who need my services more than you do. So if you'll excuse me. . .' He rolled up the sphygmomanometer, picked up her casenotes, and turned on his heel.

Suddenly repentant, Sam called after him, 'Doctor!'

He paused. 'Yes?'

'How long do you think I'll have to stay in hospital?'

'We'll talk about that in the morning—unless you choose to discharge yourself overnight, which, speaking as your physician, I can't recommend.' His tone of voice, however, left Sam in no doubt at all that, speaking personally, he felt that for her to sign a risk form and leave the hospital was a consummation devoutly to be wished.

He had reached the door when he heard her say, 'Doctor!' again.

He spoke without turning. 'Yes?'

'I feel rather. . .strange.'

So this was the next act in her little play! He almost ignored her and walked on, but clinical instinct cautioned him to make sure. He turned. She was sitting up in bed, as he had left her, but her face was white as a sheet.

In three swift strides he was beside her. As his arm went round her shoulders, her head dropped forward and she slumped against his chest. He held her for a moment or two, then lowered her carefully on to the pillow. One hand reached for her pulse as the other raised an eyelid to ascertain the state of her pupils. He found himself wishing he had a third hand to ring the bell and summon Sister. But that was ridiculous, he admonished himself. Whatever had happened to his famed clinical detachment? There was no need for panic stations. All the signs proclaimed this to be nothing more than a simple faint. And she was already coming out of it, opening her eyes and murmuring something.

'Just take it slowly,' he said, holding her wrist to check her pulse yet again.

'I'm sorry about that. . . I must have. . .'

'You fainted—nothing to worry about. Just reaction, following the accident.' He was reassuring himself as much as her, and being uncharacteristically verbose about it. 'I shouldn't have given you such a lengthy assessment. But you seemed. . .' Stow it, Tony! he told himself.

'I'll check your blood-pressure,' he said abruptly.

Sam closed her eyes as he applied the cuff to her arm. She still looked very pale and her breathing was shallow. He really had been an unthinking fool; he could have— should have —left his full assessment until she had recovered a bit more from the accident.

'As I expected,' he said, rolling up the cuff again, 'your BP is low. And, being a nurse,' a smile flickered, 'you'll want to know just how low. It's 105 on 65. So I suggest you remain very quiet for the rest of the day.'

He reached for the bell. 'I'll hand you over to Sister. I'm confident there's nothing in your condition, either inside or outside,' again his lips twitched briefly, 'for you to worry about.'

'I *am* sorry,' Sam repeated, and he knew that this time she wasn't apologising for having fainted.

He looked down at her with one eyebrow raised, saw the appeal in her eyes, and relented.

'Apology accepted. But no repeat performances, please! You know how easily we doctors bruise!'

She gave a tiny chuckle. 'Don't I just! And I promise.'

Sister arrived at that moment and the doctor gave her a brief résumé of his examination and of Sam's episode of syncope, making no attempt to prevent Sam overhearing. He ended by saying, 'No sedation or analgesics pro tem, Sister. Oh, and our patient is a nurse—quite a knowledgeable one, I gather. I've no doubt she'll fill you in on anything I've omitted to tell you.'

His tone was dry, but his smile reached his eyes this time. And yes, those lines in his cheeks did deepen when he smiled.

Perhaps he's human after all, Sam thought, and smiled back.

Tony went off to the duty-room to write up his notes. When he had finished he sat for a moment, gazing into space, wondering what Sister Benson would say if she found in the notes on this patient one last observation—'Intermittent unilateral right-sided dimple.'

He smiled, then the smile became a frown, and as he walked along to check on his patient in Room Four he looked as though some unresolved problem was weighing heavily on his mind.

CHAPTER TWO

'So, you're a nurse—from England. Been working over here?'

'No, just holidaying.'

'Mmm. Well, you won't be enjoying your holiday for a while, I'm afraid. How are you feeling now?'

'Much better. I'm sorry I fainted.'

'Quite understandable. Just reaction to the accident—a bit of delayed shock.'

As she talked, Sister's hands were busy, pulling the blue hospital gown into place about Sam's shoulders, straightening the bedclothes, pouring liquid into a glass.

'Drink some of this,' she ordered.

'This' was cool, sweet and refreshing.

'That's nice! Thanks.'

'Are you feeling hungry yet?'

'Actually I could eat a horse. There can't be too much wrong with me.'

'A little scrambled egg for lunch, I think. And some jelly might give you a bit of energy.'

A nurse Sam might be, but to Sister Benson she was, first and foremost, a patient. Feeling as she did, Sam was happy to have it so.

'One more pillow, I think. Can you lean forward a touch?'

Sam obliged, and Sister patted and prodded the pillows until she was satisfied they were how she wanted them.

'Right! An hour's rest before lunch for you, I think.'

Sam was beginning to realise that there was nothing

14

indecisive about Sister's 'I think'. What Sister thought inevitably became fact, and sooner rather than later.

'Now,' Sister was saying, 'is there anyone who'll be wondering what's become of you?'

'I'm on my way to Adelaide. I was planning to stay there for a week or two, but I hadn't made any bookings. I do have an uncle in Perth. I spent the last few days with him.'

'I'll make sure he's contacted. The accident's been in the news, so he may be anxious. Do you have a phone number?'

Sam looked around her. 'In my handbag. . .'

'They're still trying to sort out which luggage is whose. Now that we know your name, you'll have yours soon. Just give me your uncle's name and address.'

Sam obliged, although she was hazy about the name of her uncle's street. As Sister jotted down the information, Sam asked, 'How bad was the accident, Sister?'

It was a question she had been longing to ask ever since regaining consciousness, but until now there had not been an opportunity. The doctor's attitude had certainly not encouraged any questions.

'Bad enough,' said Sister, 'but it could have been a lot worse, with a whole busload of passengers involved. There were no deaths—some fairly serious injuries, though.'

Sam nodded soberly. 'You must be busy, Sister. Please don't worry any more about me. I only wish I could help.'

Sister smiled. 'Try and forget that you're a nurse for a while. Close your eyes and have that rest before lunch arrives.'

'First, can I ask. . .?' Sam looked across the room. The curtains around the bed opposite were drawn back now and the bed was empty, stripped of its linen. 'When I

woke up the first time there was a girl in the bed over
there. Is she. . .?'

'Deepening coma. She's been flown to Adelaide for
more tests and a CAT scan.'

Sam nodded her understanding. She had a dozen
other questions awaiting answers, but Sister was already
on her way out of the room.

Sam lay on her pillows, admitting to herself that she
did indeed feel more like a patient than a nurse just now.
Every muscle in her body was sore and her leg throbbed
badly. She gingerly felt the bandage around her right
thigh, trying to assess the extent of the laceration
beneath it. She should have insisted that the doctor tell
her more about it. After all, it was her body, not his.

That turned her thoughts to the doctor. If only his
manners matched his looks! A pity he didn't smile more
often. Perhaps he did—with other people. Despite the
slight thawing in his attitude to her after she had fainted,
she still was convinced he had taken a dislike to her. She
couldn't imagine why. But, however badly he'd behaved,
she shouldn't have pulled the stunt she had on him. . .

Suddenly she was overwhelmed by a confusion of
feelings of guilt, resentment and self-pity. She recognised
them for what they were—post-trauma blues—and
decided to try not to think at all until she could think
rationally. She would take Sister's advice and have a
catnap, if her aches and pains permitted. She closed her
eyes—and found herself reliving the last few hours, in
vivid Technicolor. She forced her mind back, beyond the
accident.

Was it only six weeks since she had left Sydney? She
had travelled north, up through the beaches of
Queensland to Cairns, where she had met up with a
group of travellers from London. They had all crossed
the Outback by bus to Darwin, where she and another
nurse had purchased an old car. In that, they had

explored the Kakadu region, with its lush wetlands, water buffalo and crocodiles, then taken their time travelling down the desolate coast of Western Australia to Perth, where Sam had stayed a few days with her uncle. The bus trip to Adelaide was to have been the easy part!

The accident had happened in the early hours of the morning, when most of the passengers had been sleeping or dozing. They had left the Nullarbor Plain behind them and were heading east still, across flat, uninteresting country.

She could remember hearing the roar of a semi-trailer, approaching from the opposite direction. She knew it was close—much too close. The bus had swerved, skidded, then rolled over and over, down an embankment. In the darkness, people were screaming. The inside of the bus had seemed full of flying debris. Then, as if in slow motion, everything had stopped moving. Sam had found she was wedged against a shattered window. She'd moved her limbs tentatively. Thank goodness they'd all responded. She'd begun to pull herself upright and somehow, in the darkness and confusion, had struggled out of the wreckage. Several other passengers had done the same, and were wandering about, dazed and shocked, in the moonlight. Instinctively she'd known she should be doing something for those still trapped in the bus. One of the party of young footballers, who had joined the bus in Kalgoorlie, walked past her. He'd looked as wobbly on his legs as she felt on hers, but he'd responded immediately when she said to him, 'Come on—we must do something!'

The rest was a hazy memory. She thought. . .she hoped. . .she had done some good before she'd passed out—to wake up later in this hospital bed.

She must find out about the others. That nice soldier she had laughed and joked with on the long journey east from Perth—she couldn't remember seeing him after the accident. And the family with three children, the youngest a three-month-old baby girl. She vaguely remembered carrying the baby from the bus as the footballer helped the mother. The driver—he'd looked pretty bad, slumped over the wheel. He'd been such a livewire, keeping the passengers entertained with his racy commentary and stories about the places they were passing through. That story of his about the family whose car had been buzzed by a UFO while crossing the Nullarbor. . . Sam thought if there were any place on earth aliens from outer space would choose to land it would surely be the Nullarbor Plain. Nullarbor—meaning 'no trees'—an appropriate name for the miles of endless, treeless desert, bathed in eerie moonlight. . .

Sam awoke from a confused, nightmarish dream. A nurse was in the room. She dumped an armload of clean linen on the table beside the other bed, then turned and smiled at Sam. She looked a little younger than Sam, with blonde straight hair tucked up under her cap, and lively blue eyes.

'Sorry! I didn't mean to wake you.'

'I'm glad you did.' Sam shivered slightly, the aftermath of her dream still with her.

The nurse seemed to understand. 'It must have been quite a smash! By the way, my name's Louise. I hear you're a nurse too.'

Sam was not surprised that that piece of information had become common knowledge in the hospital. It would have been passed on quickly, simply because it was embarrassing for staff to talk to a patient in layman's terms, only to discover later that the patient too was a nurse or a doctor. Sam had been in that situation herself more than once, and knew just how it felt. She cringed mentally to think about the prank she had pulled on the doctor this morning. Perhaps he hadn't deserved it after all. Perhaps he had problems of his own—a terminally ill patient, a nagging wife, sick kids. . .

Sam being a nurse, Louise told her what she wanted to know about the other passengers on the bus. The driver and a man seated just behind him had fared worst. They, and the girl in a coma, had been flown to Adelaide by air ambulance. Several people with minor injuries had been treated in Outpatients and were staying overnight at the only motel in town, with instructions to call in if their symptoms worsened. The hospital had managed to find beds for the others, although, Louise told Sam with a chuckle, two footballers had ended up in Maternity.

Sam laughed too, then said, 'I know it sounds like a cliché and a rather belated one at that, but—where am I?'

'At Wirrando Bay. Those windows face east and overlook Spencer Gulf. In the other direction are the Eyre Peninsula, the Nullarbor Plain and Western Australia, in that order. But you'll know that—it's where you came from, isn't it?'

'Yes. And thanks—it's good to have my bearings again. One feels very disorientated waking up in a strange place.'

'I can imagine.'

'Wirrando—it's a pretty name. What does it mean?'

'It's Aboriginal—something to do with wallabies and gum trees.'

'It's a small town?'

'Quite small.'

'Have you got staff to cope with emergencies like this?'

'Not normally, but several retired nurses live in the district and come in if they're needed.' Louise chuckled. 'There'll be a few farmers getting their own dinners tonight!'

'And how many doctors. . .?'

'Just the two—well, one and a half, really. Charles Welsh is virtually retired and spends most of his time with his son and his family in Whyalla. He only comes down when Tony—that's Tony Larsen—needs an assistant in Theatre or has time off. Nice guys, both of them.'

Louise went back to her bedmaking. She mitred a corner expertly, smoothed the quilt, lined up three pillows in a flash and said, 'I must fly. Nice to have had a chat. See you later.'

So, thought Sam, when Louise had departed, his name is Tony Larsen. And he's a 'nice guy'. Perhaps she'd made up her mind about him too precipitately, but she wouldn't be around to see if he improved on acquaintance. She sighed and closed her eyes wearily.

Lunch came and went. Sam dozed away the rest of the day. Just after they had settled her down for the night and switched off all but one dim light, she heard Dr Larsen's voice. He was talking to the night sister outside her room. She waited for him to come in, but the voices faded away down the corridor. Instead of feeling relieved to know that he didn't think her condition warranted a visit, she was resentful that he had ignored her.

Sam had had very little illness in her life but, being a nurse, she knew that the feelings of resentment and maudlin self-pity that had afflicted her on and off throughout the day were typical of post-trauma patients. Tomorrow, after a good night's sleep, she should be back to something approaching her normal optimistic self. On the positive side, Louise had been a bright spot in the day, and Sister Benson was nice. . .

Sam was sponged, dressed in a pretty blue nightdress that Louise had thoughtfully dropped in for her, and propped up on several pillows with a breakfast tray on

her overbed table, when Dr Larsen, accompanied by
Sister Benson, appeared early the next morning.

He seemed to bring with him a breath of fresh air and
looked much more relaxed than he had yesterday.

He greeted Sam with a cheerful, 'Hello, there!'

'Good morning,' Sam replied, and couldn't resist
adding, 'You look as though you've just come in from an
early morning gallop.'

He raised his eyebrows in surprise.

'The lady is clairvoyant. Or should I say "full marks
for being an observant nurse." You're not doing too
badly for yourself this morning,' he added, indicating
her breakfast tray, with its egg and bacon, toast and
marmalade, and a small silver tea service.

'Sister thought I could manage a little more susten-
ance this morning,' Sam told him, with the tiniest flutter
of an eyelid on the side remote from Sister.

'Did she now!' he said, and a responsive twinkle in his
eye showed that he had not missed her allusion to
Sister's favourite mannerism of speech.

Sister smiled, sublimely unaware.

'Well, there's nothing worse than cold bacon and egg,'
the doctor said, 'so I'll let you get on with it. Is there
any reason for me to call back later and check on this
patient, Sister?'

'None whatever. You saw for yourself how soundly
she slept last night, and she seems to be well and truly
on the mend today,' Sister assured him, sensing that he
was disappointed at not having an excuse to come back
and see more of this young lady. In one way that was
not surprising, Sister thought. Samantha Hayes certainly
was a very attractive lass. On the other hand, she would
have thought Tony had enough problems with females
at the present time to last him a lifetime.

Tony was saying, 'Then, unless you have any reason
to call me earlier, Sister, I'll see Samantha again

tomorrow, and possibly send her on her way, though
I'm not entirely satisfied with that trigeminal nerve, for
all we agreed yesterday that it was unaffected. I thought
I detected a small tic in that area this morning.'

'Oh?' Sister looked at Sam closely and Sam smiled
guiltily at Tony.

'It was a very transitory tic,' she assured him.

'I rather thought so. Well, in that case, goodbye for
now.'

His smile transformed his rather serious face, but this
morning Sam saw something she had missed yesterday.
Then she had been aware of hostility only, but today, in
spite of his smile, she thought there was sadness in his
face as well.

When she was alone again she tackled her breakfast
absentmindedly, barely aware that it was now
lukewarm.

She had discovered quite a lot more about the doctor
this morning, she realised, and began enumerating her
findings.

Yesterday she had thought him dour and sombre, but
she knew now that he had a sense of humour, because
he had been very quick to pick up her allusion to Sister
Benson's little quirk of speech, and to come back at her
with that comment about her 'tic'.

He didn't harbour grudges, and she was glad about
that. If he did, he would still have been touchy on the
subject of her trigeminal nerve and would have avoided
referring to it.

And she knew for sure, now, that he was an outdoor
man as well as a country doctor. Horses, early-morning
gallops, wide-open spaces—they were all there, in his
eyes and in his face.

She was still puzzled about two things—his attitude
to her yesterday, and that lurking sadness behind his
eyes. She could fill in some of the time that lay heavy on

her hands this morning by thinking about those things. But she would never know the answers, because tomorrow, or the next day at the latest, she would be discharged, to continue her journey to Adelaide, and would never see him again.

Suddenly despondent, she put down her cup of luke-warm tea and pushed the tray away from her.

After a time, she smiled. He *had* called in to see her last night, after all, even though she had been too soundly asleep to know anything about it.

All things considered, Louise probably wasn't too far off course in calling him 'a nice guy'.

CHAPTER THREE

SAM fossicked out a mirror from her bag and surveyed herself critically. Her hair was a mess and her face was unusually pale, but she thought it didn't look too bad against her dark hair. 'An interesting pallor', they would probably call it in books.

She could see glimpses of the sea now that she was sitting up, through the awning blinds which were drawn against the morning sun. The bed opposite her remained empty and the nurses who popped in and out were obviously too busy to stay chatting. By the time morning tea came at ten o'clock, she knew why so many patients said plaintively, 'It's such a long day, Nurse.'

The cup of tea gave her a spurt of energy and she decided it was time she did something positive to speed her recovery. Across the room was the door to an en-suite bathroom. If she could demonstrate that her legs were capable of carrying her there and back, perhaps, later in the day, the powers-that-be, alias Sister Benson, might let her take a shower and wash her hair.

She pulled herself upright and gingerly swung her legs over the side of the bed. A sharp pain jabbed at her temple. She sat still, waiting for it to pass, and noticed that her left leg too was sporting some spectacular bruises. Her legs and head had obviously taken the brunt of the trauma. And, of course, her emotions!

Well, it's now or never, she thought, and slid forward, taking her weight on her left leg as it touched the floor. So far, so good. She let go of the bed and ventured a step away from it. A searing pain shot up her right thigh, and she spun around with arms outflung, grasping the edge of the bed to keep herself from falling. Louise, walking in at that moment, was at her side in an instant, a firm supporting hand under her elbow, easing her back on to the bed.

'I didn't know you were a ballerina,' she grinned. 'The Dying Swan, I presume?'

Sam groaned in frustration.

'Hurts, does it?' asked Louise cheerfully. Sam wondered whether all Australian nurses were so sadistic.

'Yes,' she replied, through gritted teeth.

'Serves you right! *You* should know that patients must wait for permission before they go walkabout.'

'I *do* know, but I'm bored out of my brain and I don't want to lie in that bed forever. What about exercising a little of that compassion we nurses are famous for and helping me get moving?'

Louise cocked her head on one side and said, 'Brains. . .charm. . . I'm not so sure about compassion. *We* were always warned against having too much of it, in case we became emotional wrecks ourselves.'

Sam looked at Louise's laughing face. 'I don't think you're in any imminent danger of that happening,' she informed her. 'Now, do you think you could help me over to the bathroom?'

'Not without Sister's say-so. But hang on and I'll go and ask her.'

Louise was only away a short time, and when she reappeared she was brandishing a silver walking-stick and carrying an armful of magazines which she deposited on Sam's overbed table.

'Sister thinks a *little* compassion is in order. I'm allowed to help you to the bathroom and back, if you promise not to break any more of our rules in future.'

Sam placed a hand, with two fingers conspicuously crossed, over her heart, and said, 'I promise!'

Ten minutes later she was sinking thankfully back on to her pillows.

'So this is how patients feel,' she said, and exhaled a long breath.

Louise grinned, straightened the bedclothes, and handed Sam a magazine. It was a *New Idea* with a picture of Princess Diana on the front cover. 'Then make like a patient and read about Fergie's new house, or whatever, until lunchtime. That is, if you Brits are as infatuated with your Royals as we are over here.'

'Some are, some aren't. And thanks.'

'Any time. But no more ballet without buzzing first, OK?' Louise flitted away.

Sam lay, considering with interest the fact that she really didn't have the energy even to open the magazine, and that it was quite as exhausting being a patient as being a nurse. In future she would be more sympathetic towards her patients. Which might not necessarily be in their best interest, she thought wryly.

She soon became aware of an unusual amount of activity in the hospital. There was a procession of footsteps past her door, some rapid, some slow. She tried to identify the owners of voices she heard in the corridor and whether the sound of wheels on the polished floor was that of trolleys or of wheelchairs. Cars came and went on the gravel driveway below her window. Twice an ambulance passed by.

Familiar as she was with hospital routine, and assisted by snatches of conversation she was able to decipher, she soon realised that the bus passengers who had spent the night in the motel were being brought in for check-ups prior to being discharged. It sounded as though some of the hospital patients were being released as well.

Sam knew how much work all this would cause. The paperwork alone would be a formidable task for a small hospital. It felt so frustrating to have to lie here doing nothing.

By mid-afternoon, peace prevailed again. Louise came in and sank into an armchair, spreadeagling her arms and legs. 'Phew!' she sighed. 'I'm glad we don't have to cope with a major VA every week—though it did liven the old place up a bit.'

Sam grinned at her. 'What was that we were saying about compassionate nurses? Speaking of which, has anything been heard about the bus driver and the other two who were flown to Adelaide yesterday?'

'Everybody has been asking the same question, so Matron rang the Royal Adelaide Hospital to enquire. Hayley is still in a coma but is stable, and the others are "satisfactory".'

'That's good to know. I gather from the mild panic I've been hearing that you've sent some of the others on their way.'

Louise nodded, sighed and stood up. 'And now we have about a dozen beds to make up.' A nurse popped her head around the door and Louise called to her, 'Just coming, Jonesy. See you later, Samantha.'

It took Sam several minutes of gazing at the ceiling to rationalise the sense of disappointment that descended on her, following Louise's departure, because none of the passengers had looked in to say 'Hi' or 'Goodbye' to her before leaving. She finally did manage to convince herself that, if forty or so of them had tried to contact all the others before leaving, there would have been more than just mild chaos in the hospital. And of course, having survived what could have been a tragic accident, everyone would be thinking first and foremost about getting home to family and friends.

Family and friends! The realisation hit Sam suddenly of how many thousands of miles lay between her and her family. Her parents didn't know she had been in an accident, and would still be imagining her tripping with carefree abandon around Australia. It was much better that they didn't know, she told herself. They would only worry, and after all, she'd be on her way again in a day or two.

All the same, she had a sudden fierce longing to talk to her mother, who somehow always managed to come up with just the right blend of sympathy and common sense for any situation.

Her father was a lecturer in history at Oxford University and they lived in a big, rambling old house in the Chiltern Hills. He had not approved of his only daughter becoming a nurse.

'Crazy idea! No need to work! Stay home and help your mother. Or do a course or something!'

'That's what I intend doing—a course in nursing,' Sam had told him.

'Hurrumph!'

As for traipsing all over Australia! Dreadful place! Deserts, snakes, crocodiles! If Sam rang and told him about the accident, he'd say, 'I told you so!' and add, 'I'll go and get your mother,' knowing that from her mother Sam would get the sympathy she needed.

Tears brimmed suddenly and overflowed down Sam's cheeks. She closed her eyes, wondering how much longer she would be the victim of these attacks of the blues.

'Do you need something for pain?' a voice asked.

Sam's eyes flew open. Dr Larsen was standing over her, looking down at her. She shook her head and reached for a tissue.

'No. I'm just feeling sorry for myself.'

'Do you usually react to setbacks this way?'

Sam gasped. The man was unsufferable! Nice guy? How could anyone think that? She doubted he so much as knew the meaning of the word 'empathy'. If he did, it was obviously no more than a theoretical concept to him. She dashed her tissue across her face and glared at him, not trusting herself to speak.

'Sister tells me you took yourself for a walk this morning.'

So *that* was what was biting him! She had dared to act on her own initiative, without waiting for his permission. Before she could think of a suitable retort, he continued, 'I'd like you to come for a short walk with me now.'

He would, would he? Just to let her know who was boss, no doubt! She opened her mouth to say, And if I refuse? but he didn't give her the chance.

'Do you have a dressing-gown?' he asked.

'Yes. But I'm not sure I feel like going for a walk at present, thank you,' she said loftily.

She might as well not have spoken.

'Where is it?' he asked.

The surge of energy that had been created by her anger abated suddenly, leaving her feeling tired and drained, her brief rebellion over.

'Louise hung some of my clothes in the wardrobe,' she muttered.

He walked over to the wardrobe and came back carrying her dark blue towelling robe. It was far from new and not at all glamorous, having seen her through her nursing training as well as her travels of the last two months. But why worry? She had not the least desire to impress Tony Larsen. Listlessly she held out a hand to take the gown.

He shook his head and said peremptorily, 'Sit up!'

He seemed determined to make this as difficult as possible. Tight-lipped, Sam sat up, then, with his assistance, slid her arms, one after the other, into the sleeves of the gown. He held out a hand, but she ignored it for a moment, before, tacitly admitting her need of assistance, she grasped his arm just above the wrist.

Allowing her plenty of time, he helped her to turn and

lower her legs over the side of the bed. She was careful
not to let him see how sore she felt, or that her head
spun momentarily, but he seemed to know without being
told, and allowed her to sit quietly until she gave a slight
nod. Then he placed his free forearm under hers and
drew her into a standing position, continuing to steady
her as she pulled her gown into place and tied the sash
around her waist. Next he slid a foot beneath the bed
and brought out her slippers, and waited while she
slipped her feet into them.

Sam had to admit that his technique in assisting a stiff
and sore patient out of bed had been flawless. In fact,
she couldn't have done it better herself. She gave a
reluctant smile and murmured, 'Thank you.'

They began a slow progress across the room, and
when she was sure her legs were not gong to play her
false she said loftily, 'I take it the object of this exercise
is to allow you to assess how far I've recovered?'

'Not at all. I thought a little social life might brighten
up your ideas.'

A little social life? Sam cocked her head to look up at
him, but aborted the attempt as her head spun madly.

She clung more tightly to his arm and said drily,
'Sounds fun, but I must warn you I'm not feeling
particularly gregarious at the moment. I'd rather, if you
don't mind, just go back to bed.'

He pressed her arm more firmly against his side and
she could feel the ripple of muscles as he walked.

'Just for once, accept that your medical adviser might
know what's best for you,' he told her.

They were out of the room now and progressing along
the corridor, albeit very slowly. Sam smiled to herself as
it occurred to her that there was something quite domestic about the scenario. To look at them, the doctor
might have been any husband, helping his wife on the
road to recovery. Did he have a wife? she wondered. If

he treated other women as he did his female patients, chances were he was still single, unless some woman was foolish enough to settle for good looks and put up with boorish behaviour.

'You're doing fine,' he said, and smiled down at her encouragingly. She promptly felt a heel.

After a few more steps he paused and flung open a door. Sam assumed they had arrived at their destination, but she found herself looking into a gleaming operating theatre.

'This is where we patch up visiting English nurses, et al.,' he said. She looked around with interest, then nodded, and they continued on their way. Sam suspected, now, that he was taking her to have afternoon tea with the nurses in their staff-room. If she had been feeling better she would have enjoyed that, but, in her present condition, she was not so sure.

'We're almost there,' he said. Then, a minute later, 'Here we are.' He knocked on a door.

Sam thought that the female voice which called 'Come in!' sounded vaguely familiar. Tony opened the door without relinquishing his hold on Sam's arm, and guided her inside.

'Samantha! What a lovely surprise!'

It was Eleanor Purvis, the mother of the family who had been on the bus from Perth. Her eyes were shining and she was clearly delighted to see Sam. She had been holding her baby in her arms, but, as Sam approached, she laid her on the bed in front of her, saying, 'I'm sorry I can't get out of bed. But come here and let me give you a big hug.'

Sam tried to hide her surprise at the enthusiasm of Eleanor's welcome. They had all been on friendly terms on the bus and Sam had helped amuse the children from time to time, but there had been nothing to warrant the warmth that was in Eleanor's voice now.

Tony Larsen, seeing Sam's bewilderment, smiled enigmatically and released his hold of her arm, allowing her to move forward and receive Eleanor's 'big hug'. Sam returned the embrace and, as she straightened up, heard Eleanor say, 'Eric and I are so very grateful. We can never hope to repay you for what you did.'

Sam looked up at Tony Larsen, who could not suppress a chuckle at her puzzled expression.

'I suspect Samantha is suffering from some degree of amnesia still,' he explained to Eleanor. Then, to Sam, he said, 'According to a number of witnesses, Jodi, Eleanor's young daughter here, owes her life to you.'

Sam looked stunned. 'I have a vague recollection. . . I can remember her crying. . .and carrying her. : .'

Tony moved forward and stroked the baby's hand. 'You climbed back into the bus, freed her from her carry-cot and took her outside—just minutes before a heavy suitcase, dislodged by an injured passenger trying to clamber out of the wreckage, toppled down—right where she'd been lying. She'd almost certainly have been killed if she'd still been there.'

'Well. . . I'm glad. . .' Overwhelmed, Sam stood looking down at the chubby, very much alive baby, kicking and gurgling in her pale yellow jumpsuit on the bed.

She had actually saved a life! 'So very glad,' she repeated softly. Suddenly the baby on the bed had become very special to her. She reached out her arms.

'May I?' she asked.

Dr Larsen interposed with a smile. 'Only if you sit down first. We don't want some dizzy nurse dropping her now, after all she's been through,' he said.

Sam lowered herself into the armchair beside the bed as Tony picked the baby up and carefully placed her in her arms. She gazed down at her in wonderment. Then, not at all ashamed this time of the tears in her eyes, she looked up at Dr Larsen, suddenly understanding why he had brought her here. And she had thought him callous and unfeeling, lacking in empathy for his patients!

'Thank you,' she said simply.

He had been standing looking down at her and the baby, and there was something in his eyes as Sam glanced up that caused her heart to thump suddenly. But the next second she wondered whether she had imagined it, because his face became blank, as though a shutter had fallen. He made a gruff, non-committal sort of sound and said, 'I must go—there are patients I need to see. Ring for a nurse when you're ready to return to your room.'

He made his escape, closed the door behind him, and stood in the corridor, taking a deep breath or two.

He felt quite sure that if Samantha Hayes stayed around here for long it would spell trouble for him. Sure, she had looked like a Madonna, sitting there holding the baby, with tears in her eyes and her fingers gently stroking its cheeks. But it wasn't as a Madonna he was thinking of her at this moment, and he had enough complications in his life already without adding to them.

His hand sketched an impatient, dismissive gesture and he turned and walked away along the corridor, wondering why he had let the girl get under his skin, as she had done from the word go. The best thing for all concerned would be for him to discharge her—send her on her way as soon as possible. Tomorrow morning he'd speak to Sister, organise it. . .

He waited for the sense of relief which should have followed the making of that decision but, for some reason, it didn't come. Whatever, he knew it to be a wise decision. In fact, in the circumstances, the only possible one.

CHAPTER FOUR

As IT happened, when Dr Larsen suggested that Samantha Hayes be discharged, Sister Benson had other, very definite ideas.

It was next morning, and she and Dr Larsen were standing one on either side of Sam's bed—discussing her as though she were not there, Sam thought indignantly.

'Tomorrow is much too soon!' declared Sister. 'Much too soon! She still has her sutures in.'

She could go to OPD at Royal Adelaide to have them removed,' said the doctor stubbornly.

Neither showed any sign of yielding, but Sam was prepared to put her money on Sister Benson.

'If she were going home, it would be a different matter. But to a motel in Adelaide! She's not ready for it.'

'You said you were short of beds.'

'We are, but not so much so that we have to discharge patients before they're well enough to go.'

Lying there, ignored, Sam began a slow burn. Why was Tony Larsen trying so hard to get rid of her? The bed opposite was still empty, so their bed shortage couldn't be all that acute. Certainly she had got off to a bad start with the good doctor, and she hadn't been a model patient since. But all the same, it was a bit much, being made to feel so obviously *persona non grata*. As well as being angry, she felt absurdly disappointed.

'Do I have any say about this?' she asked pointedly.

Tony Larsen looked down at her and frowned, as though he had just remembered she was there. He opened his mouth, then closed it quickly. As she realised that he had been on the verge of emitting an emphatic 'No!' the speech she had been about to make died on her lips.

She had been going to say that she was quite well enough to leave hospital. Eleanor Purvis was being flown home to Adelaide tomorrow by air ambulance, so they could go together. What was more, Eleanor had told her that if ever she needed a bed in Adelaide she had only to ask.

But the idea of meekly taking herself off just because Dr Larsen wanted her gone was too galling to be indulged. She was a free agent. She could do as she liked, and it suddenly occurred to her that what she would like was to spend a few more days in Wirrando. She would convalesce here, have a look around, spend some time with Louise, who seemed to be a kindred spirit. . .

'I think I know of a way to please everyone,' she said, smiling sweetly at Dr Larsen, knowing full well that what she was about to suggest would not please him at all.

'What's that, my dear?' asked Sister.

'Since you're short of beds, I can be discharged from hospital. Then I shall spend a few days in the motel here, as the other patients did, remaining under your care, of course, Doctor, until my sutures are removed and I can travel more comfortably.'

Sister's face brightened.

'That's an excellent solution. Don't you agree, Tony?'

Tony didn't have much option but to agree. He wouldn't have missed the slight emphasis Sam had placed on the words 'I shall', and would know that she was stating her intention, not asking for his permission.

'As you like,' he responded ungraciously, and added immediately, 'Sister, we have a busy morning. We can't waste any more time.'

Inwardly fuming, Sam watched his retreating back. She gradually began to realise that, although she had won her victory, it was somewhat of a Pyrrhic one. In fact, she had cut off her nose to spite her face, because, if she *had* allowed him to pack her off to Adelaide, she would not have to see him again. And *that*, she assured herself fiercely, would have been just wonderful—just what she most wanted to happen.

A few minutes later Sister was back.

'Well, he's gone. I don't know what he was thinking about, wanting to discharge you before you're well enough! I've insisted that you're to stay here today. Tomorrow will be quite time enough for you to go to the motel.' She walked out, tut-tutting indignantly.

By noon, the veranda outside Sam's room was in shade, and she took a book and sat there for a time, but the words blurred before her eyes and she slipped in and out of a doze for an hour or so. The forecast was for a maximum temperature in the low thirties, but a slight breeze kept the heat bearable. It also brought whiffs of perfume from a group of tall, straight-trunked, lemon-scented gums away to Sam's left. Now and then a kookaburra laughed stridently. The sun sparkling on the sea was unbearably bright. She closed her eyes again.

By teatime, she could think about Tony Larsen without a spurt of indignation. By bedtime, her natural optimism had reasserted itself and she had convinced herself that her decision to stay on for a time was a wise one. She slept soundly without medication and woke next morning feeling much better.

A pretty little nurse called Beth made Sam's bed and brought in her breakfast. She had light brown skin, curly brown hair and sparkling black eyes, and Sam guessed her to be half-Aboriginal.

Beth chattered away as she worked. A somewhat

unusual situation prevailed in the hospital this morning,
and it was evidently quite to the liking of the staff on
duty. Matron had rung through to say she had a
prostrating headache and the beginning of fever. The
dreaded Shanghai flu had so far missed Wirrando, but
one of the bus victims could have brought it in and, until
her illness was diagnosed as being something else,
Matron was placing herself in isolation.

Sister Benson was on her two-day break and had left
last night to spend it with her brother, who ran a small
guesthouse in Whyalla, a couple of hours' drive away.
Had she known about Matron's illness she would almost
certainly have stayed in town, where she could be on
call, but clearly the few staff who were on duty were
confident they could manage. Sam gathered they felt
they were entitled to an easy day after the hectic
aftermath of the bus incident, and were going to make
the most of the unusual freedom from supervision.

There would not even be any doctor's round this
morning. Dr Larsen had been called out with the
ambulance to a large station some distance away. A son
of the station manager had ridden his trail bike over a
cliff. Nobody knew the extent of his injuries, but it was
probable he had spinal and brain damage. The roads
were not good and, if the lad did have spinal injuries,
the return journey would be very slow.

There was a small flurry after breakfast when a cab
arrived to take Eleanor Purvis and her baby to the
airport. If the ambulance had not been engaged elsewhere they would have been transported in that, but
Eleanor had insisted she did not want the flight delayed
until the ambulance was available and that she was
quite able to make the short journey by cab. A St John's
Ambulance volunteer was there to accompany her.

Sam walked to her door to say goodbye to Eleanor,

who squeezed her hand and repeated her invitation to
visit her at any time in Adelaide.

When Eleanor had gone, Sam wondered whether she
should have asked the cab-driver to return for her later,
to take her to the motel, but she wasn't sure whether, in
the absence of authority, she was free to discharge
herself, and she didn't want to do the wrong thing and
further antagonise Tony Larsen. She gathered up a
couple of pillows and some magazines and settled herself
in the cane armchair, in the narrow, but extending strip
of shade on the veranda. Through the open door she
could hear occasional bursts of laughter, and a couple of
times a quite impressive soprano voice broke into song.

Sam smiled. She had never nursed in a small hospital
like this one, but it certainly seemed to have a lot going
for it. She flipped through her magazine, looking up
every time a car drove by on the road fronting the
hospital. She vaguely realised she was watching for the
return of the ambulance, while knowing that it could be
some time yet before it appeared, depending, of course,
on the extent of the boy's injuries and on how much first
aid had had to be administered on the spot.

She resisted the urge to close her eyes and decided to
tackle a crossword in one of the magazines. She rarely
had any bother with crosswords, but this one had quite
a lot of clues that related to Australian or New Zealand
flora and fauna, and her progress was slow.

Louise brought her own morning tea to the veranda,
along with Sam's. She pulled up a chair and chatted
with Sam for ten minutes or so as they sipped their coffee
and ate hot buttered scones. After that, Sam took a short
walk across the lawn in front of the hospital and stood
watching some children playing on the beach. She had
barely settled back in her chair when a battered Range
Rover, covered in dust, braked in front of the hospital,
veered through the gates and came to a halt outside the

main entrance, just off to Sam's left. The driver's door was flung open and a young man in worn jeans and a checked cotton shirt raced around and pulled open the door on the passenger's side.

Sam watched with interest as a heavily pregnant woman eased herself out of the car with her husband's help. They began to move slowly towards the entrance, but before they reached it the woman stopped and bent forward, clutching her swollen abdomen.

Well advanced in labour, thought Sam, and found herself beginning to stand up to offer assistance. But the pain in her leg as she rose reminded her that she was still only a patient. Frustrating though it was, she must leave the woman to Louise, who, she knew from Beth, was the only sister on duty.

At that moment the entrance door was butted open from within, and Louise backed through it, towing a wheelchair. She stood on the other side of the woman until her contraction had passed, then helped her into the chair and they quickly disappeared into the hospital. It wouldn't be long, Sam predicted, before the staff had not one but two more patients to care for.

She returned to her magazine and made another half-hearted attempt at the crossword she had been working on. But she wasn't remotely interested in rare wallabies beginning with Q, or for that matter, in finishing the crossword at all.

She had been increasingly aware, during the time she had been in hospital, of a desire to get back to work. She had been away from nursing for far too long. The sight of that woman in labour had been the final straw. Just as soon as she was well enough to travel, she would go home and find herself a job.

'Sam!'

It was Louise, and she was looking flustered.

Knowing the condition of the patient in labour, Sam

was surprised to see her here. 'How's your mid?' she asked.

'She's well advanced—seems OK. But, Sam, I think it's a breech. She said the doctor turned it once, but she's been getting kicks where she used to before it was turned, and I'm sure I can feel a head in the fundus.'

'Have you done many breech deliveries?'

'Sam, that's just it! I'm not a midwife! I've only done my general training. I've assisted in plenty of births, but they've all been straightforward. I just don't know what to do. I can't get Tony on the two-way—they must be out with the patient—and there's no one else to call. I thought maybe you. . .'

'Louise, I can barely stand up!' protested Sam.

'But you *are* a midwife?'

'Yes, but. . .' She knew it was no use continuing to protest. Louise was clearly not going to cope on her own. This was no time to worry about a few stitches in her leg.

'Of course I'll help,' she said, then, thinking quickly, added, 'Can you get me a gown and cap? And you'd better make sure there's a stool or chair strategically placed in the labour ward. And Louise. . .'

'Yes?'

'Relax! It won't help the patient if she senses we're uptight. We'll manage.'

'You're right! I'll get back to her stat. Beth will bring you a cap and gown and give you a hand to get to the ward. And thanks a million!'

'You're welcome. . . I think!'

Louise disappeared, and Sam moved back into her room as fast as she was able, shedding her robe, her watch, her dress ring, mentally listing the possible complications and manoeuvres associated with breech births. They should get Theatre ready in case there were problems, so that, when Tony did return, he could perform a Caesar without delay, if necessary.

Then Beth arrived, and Sam quickly donned the pastel-blue gown she brought and tucked her hair up into the floral cap. She glanced at herself in the mirror and smiled.

'The disguise is complete,' she said.

'Well—almost,' Beth grinned, looking down at Sam's feet. Sam looked down too. Slippers! A dead giveaway!

'Do you have any canvas boots in the labour ward?' she asked.

'I think so—we don't often use them.'

'This is one time we do. Let's go!'

Beth helped Sam across the room, smiling as though at some small private joke. When Sam saw the wheelchair standing in the corridor, she understood.

'Go on duty in a wheelchair! Not on your life!' she protested.

'Louise said. . .' pleaded Beth.

'Trust *her* to think of everything! Oh, well! There are worse ways to travel, I guess. . .'

Sam eased herself into the chair and Beth, behind her, manoeuvred it quickly and skilfully along the corridors. Both girls were chortling with laughter. Fortunately the only person they met was a ward-maid, wielding a mop, who obviously thought this was some prank inspired by Matron's absence. She grinned broadly and moved her bucket out of the path of the chair.

The maternity wing was separated from the rest of the hospital by double swing doors. Inside, Beth pointed out the post-natal wards on the right—two single rooms and two two-bed wards. She turned left, through more swing doors, and Sam saw a small waiting-room with easy chairs and a coffee machine. Then there was an office, a workroom with benches and stock cupboards, and a utility-room with an autoclave, sterilisers, basins and trolleys.

Beth came to a halt outside a half-glass door which Sam guessed was the labour-room. Probably, in a hospital of this size, it would be a labour-cum-delivery-room.

'I'll fetch some boots,' said Beth, and scuttled away just as Louise emerged from the labour-room. She grinned when she saw Sam.

'*Sister* Hayes, I presume! Am I glad to see *you!*'

'I'm beginning to have serious doubts about this! Is there really no one we can call?' asked Sam.

'No one who can be here under two or three hours. Our best hope is that Tony will be back in time for the delivery. But if not. . .?' Louise looked at Sam anxiously.

'If not, we'll manage,' said Sam, forcing herself, for Louise's sake, to sound more confident than she felt. Normally she would have revelled in the situation. It wasn't her ability to conduct the delivery that was worrying her. Her training had been excellent and she had coped with a wide variety of midwifery situations in her district work. It was her leg and her general physical condition she was concerned about. After all, it was only three days since she'd passed out in a dead faint in Dr Larsen's arms. . . Better not to think about that.

She thrust her feet into the boots Beth was holding for her and stood up.

'Lay on, Macduff!' Making an effort to walk without limping, she followed Louise into the labour-room.

'Hello there!' Sam smiled at the woman in the bed, and the husband, who was seated beside her. Both looked tense and apprehensive.

'This is Sister Hayes, Mrs McAllister,' said Louise, and added, 'She'll be looking after you now.'

Sam plucked a mask from a container by the door and put it on, trying not to look around her and thus reveal to the patient and her husband that this was the first time she had set foot in this room.

'I'll just wash my hands and then we'll see how you're progressing.' As Sam moved over to the basin, Louise placed the patient's file on a nearby trolley, so Sam was able to peruse it as she scrubbed.

A multipara-2. That was good. For all her optimism, she wasn't sure she could have coped with the longer labour of a primip.

She dried her hands. 'Now, I want to feel your tummy—just as your doctor has done during your check-ups.' She placed her hands on the woman's abdomen, curling her fingers around the fundus. She could feel a round, hard, ballotable object between her hands—without a doubt the baby's head. Louise was right—it was a breech. She moved her hands further down, feeling with her flattened palms for the smooth hard surface of the baby's back. She wasn't able to feel it, which was quite common in breech presentations. But the collection of knobs and lumps she *could* feel was comforting, as it indicated that the baby's legs were not extended. Extended legs splinted the baby's body, making delivery even more difficult, and could also cause congenital dislocation of the hips.

Sam smiled reassuringly at Mrs McAllister. 'Everything seems fine,' she said, adding,' And here comes another contraction,' as she felt the abdomen become rigid beneath her hands. At the same instant the woman's body tensed.

'Deep breaths,' Sam said. 'In. . .and out. In. . .and out!'

She reached a hand for the foetal stethoscope, then located and listened to the baby's heartbeat. Predictably, during a contraction, it was slower than Louise's earlier recording, but it was strong and regular. With a faint

Biro cross, she marked the spot where she had heard the beat.

'That's fine. . .' she repeated. 'Keep breathing. . . In. . .and out. In. . .and out. Good girl! Now relax. You're doing really well.'

She finished her examination, finding, as she expected, that the baby's buttocks were well engaged in the pelvis. She removed a glove and washed her hands at the bowl, then explained to Annette and Henry McAllister that their baby had turned and was in the breech position again.

'But everything seems very satisfactory and there shouldn't be any problems with the delivery,' she concluded, and was amused to see that Louise was looking even more relieved than the parents, and knew that she was thinking as much of the welfare of the midwife as of the patient.

'Dr Larsen could be back in time for the birth,' Sam continued. 'But if he isn't, I'll do it.' She grinned at Louise. 'Not wishing to boast, but we midwives are as capable as most doctors when it comes to helping babies into the world.'

'How long do you think it will be, Sister?' Annette asked.

But before Sam could reply, another contraction started and Annette was gasping, 'I feel as though I want to push!'

'That's fine. Go ahead and push,' Sam told her, 'but not too hard yet,' and added, 'I don't expect you'll be long at all now.'

With Annette second staging, Sam's hopes of relaxing in a chair for a few minutes and snatching a quick cup of tea evaporated. And the odds on Dr Larsen's being back in time for the delivery had lengthened. But at least the end was in sight, and she was thankful for that. The last thing she wanted, feeling as she did, was a prolonged labour.

When Annette was resting quietly again, Sam drew Louise out into the ante-room and gave her some brief instructions on how to apply gentle pressure to Annette's fundus during the delivery so that Sam would need only to guide the baby's body gently, thereby minimising any chance of causing damage to it.

'And I think we should set up a monitor for the foetal heartbeat. She seems quite happy propped up on the bed, so the monitor shouldn't bother her too much. And tell me immediately if there's a change in the heart-rate.'

They returned to the ward. Louise set up the monitor and then stayed behind Annette, encouraging and directing her, while Sam sat on a stool at the foot of the bed. Fortunately for Sam, that was the accepted position for performing a breech delivery. Her leg was throbbing painfully already, as a result of her standing too long.

Fifteen minutes later Sam heard voices outside the labour-room door. Tony Larsen! She couldn't distinguish what he was saying, only that he was questioning Beth sharply and that Beth was answering quietly.

Sam sighed. If he'd been just five minutes earlier he could have scrubbed and taken over from her. But that was impossible now, because Annette's baby had chosen that minute to make its entrance on the scene.

Sam glanced up as Tony Larsen appeared in the doorway. He was thrusting his arms into a gown as he came, with Beth trailing behind, trying to tie the strings. His face was like a thundercloud as he reached for a mask. Sam hoped desperately for the patient's sake that he wasn't going to make a scene. She injected a warning note into her voice as she said, 'Annette's been doing very well, Doctor. Just another one or two contractions and it'll all be over.'

She was pleased to see that he wiped the frown from

his face before moving around to where Annette and Henry could see him. 'That's good!' he said. 'Hello, Annette, Hi, Henry.'

He talked to them for a moment or two, then walked down and stood behind Sam, looking over her shoulder. She knew he was assessing the situation, but he said nothing—she wouldn't have had time to answer him, anyway, because she was too busy covering with warm towels the small body she was supporting in her hands, and hoping that the baby wouldn't take its first breath before its head appeared.

When she could, she glanced round and caught Tony Larsen's eye significantly. As she was the officiating midwife, it was her prerogative to tell the parents the sex of their child, but in this instance she was more than happy to waive the privilege.

He caught her meaning, nodded slightly and said, 'Well, you lucky people, you have a baby girl. That means you've got your pigeon pair. Just give us another minute and I'll be able to tell you what colour hair she's got, whether it's red like. . .'

His voice trailed away, but he quickly covered his lapse by saying, 'Now, what's the young feller's name? Of course—Pete.'

Sam knew that his hesitation had occurred when, glancing down, he had seen that the baby's unborn head was extended, instead of being nicely flexed on its chest. The head being extended made its delivery more difficult and complications more likely. Sam was now in the process of remedying the situation. Her right hand was on the baby's upward-facing back, her fingers curled over its tiny shoulders. With her left hand and forearm supporting the baby's body, she had gently inserted a finger into its mouth and was very carefully drawing its head down on to its chest.

She knew Tony Larsen must be suffering agonies of

frustration at having to stand and watch, but there was
no alternative. He was behaving very well, she thought,
not so much as offering a word of advice. And, once the
head was safely delivered, he even said a quiet, 'Well
done!' to Sam, before telling the parents, 'No red hair
this time—dark, if anything. In just a moment you can
have your first cuddle.'

Sam had the baby on her lap and was quickly clearing
its mouth of mucus before holding an oxygen mask near
its face. The baby gasped, emitted a tentative, experi-
mental squawk, then opened her mouth and gave voice
to a loud protest at the treatment she had been receiving.

Sam wrapped her in a napkin and stood up to show
her to her parents. As she did so, her right leg came into
sharp contact with the hard metal end of the bed. She
drew in a quick breath, but forced herself not to wince.
Fortunately, everyone seemed to be watching the mother
and baby, and Sam had time to recover a little. But she
felt faint and weak and knew she couldn't carry on any
longer. She handed the baby to Louise and turned to
Tony Larsen.

'Will you do the third stage?' she asked.

Of course. I'll wash up.' He moved over to the bowl.

Louise was still by the bed, supporting the baby while
Annette stroked its head wonderingly. Sam caught
Louise's eye and signalled her intention to depart. Louise
nodded.

Beth saw their signals. Throughout the delivery she
had been watching Sam anxiously, and had seen what
no one else had seen—Sam catch her leg on the end of
the bed. She moved immediately to Sam's side and,
though she did not actually take her arm, she was there,
ready for any contingency, as Sam left the ward.

Once the door closed behind them, she guided Sam to
a chair and helped her lower herself into it. Sam could
feel a deadly weakness in her limbs and an ominous

buzzing in her head. She prayed that she wasn't going to faint again. She was not aware of time passing before Beth was beside her, holding a glass of ice-cold water to her lips. She had a few sips and breathed, 'Thanks! I think the worst is over now.'

'Regardless, you're going back to bed—stat!'

The wheelchair was waiting, a folded blanket on its seat. As Beth helped Sam to stand up and remove her soiled labour ward gown, she groaned, 'Oh, no!' and stared down, appalled, at Sam's right leg.

Sam too looked down, and saw the cause of Beth's concern—bright red blood, seeping through her nightgown.

'Sit down there and don't move,' Beth ordered.

'Don't tell Dr Larsen. . .please!'

Beth hesitated, then shrugged resignedly. 'It's probably as much as my job's worth, but OK.'

She sped away and returned with a thick pad of cotton-wool which she was removing from its sterile linen cover. She also had a baby's terry-towelling napkin, and two huge safety-pins. She applied the pad quickly to the blood-soaked bandage on Sam's thigh and improvised the napkin into an additional bandage which she wrapped firmly around the leg, fastening it with the safety-pins.

Then she stood back, surveyed her handiwork, and chuckled. 'What else—in a maternity unit?' She tucked the blanket around Sam. 'Right! Let's go!'

There was no laughter on the return journey to Sam's room. Sam's only desire was to get back to bed—Beth's, to get her there without further mishap.

When Sam was snuggling thankfully under her blankets, Beth slipped out and returned almost immediately with another nurse. Together they peered at the improvised dressing on Sam's leg and came to the conclusion that there was no further haemorrhage.

'I'll go back and make sure Dr Larsen comes to see you as soon as he's finished in the labour ward,' Beth said.

Sam could have told her that wasn't necessary. She was quite sure he would come without being asked, and that he would have things to say to her that she didn't particularly want to hear.

She didn't have to wait long.

Ten minutes later he appeared and stood, ominously silent, watching as Beth cautiously removed the layers of bandage from Sam's leg. When the wound was exposed, he took one look at it and exploded.

'Of all the stupid, foolhardy things to do!'

Sam hadn't expected sympathy, but this was too much! She blinked back the tears that sprang to her eyes, expecting another reproof for being weak.

'I don't see that I had much alternative,' she retorted, and was furious that her voice broke into a sob on the last word.

'What if you hadn't been here? Don't you think the staff would have managed somehow? What makes *you* think you know it all, that you're so indispensable. . .?'

'But I *was* here. If I'd refused to help and anything had gone wrong I'd never have forgiven myself.'

'But with a leg like that! Multiple lacerations! Charles had a fine old job suturing it. And now. . .!'

Sam managed to keep a hold on her fragile equilibrium as she retorted, 'That, may I point out, is the first indication I've had that my wound was not a simple laceration. Perhaps if. . .someone. . .had had the professional courtesy to tell me just what state my leg was in, I might not have done what I did.' She paused, then added staunchly, 'But I doubt it!'

Given the same situation again, she would, she knew, do exactly as she had done today. And a doctor should have been the first to understand that.

Dr Larsen's only response was to grunt and take a few more pokes around the edges of the wound. Then he straightened up and removed his mask, gesturing for Beth to cover the wound with a sterile dressing.

'It's a resuturing job. You realise that?'

'Yes.'

'All right under a local?'

'Of course.'

He turned to Beth. 'Have someone set up a trolley in the small theatre. And call in Gillian. I'll be there in thirty minutes. In the meantime, I think the patient might need a little nourishment.'

He smiled. It was a fleeting smile, but a smile, nevertheless. Sam, inordinately thankful for small mercies, felt her own indignation begin to subside.

'I'm sorry,' she said, adding quickly, 'but don't get me wrong—I'm only sorry for the bother I'm causing you, not that I helped with the mid.'

He grinned down at her. 'Much as I hate to admit it, I do understand. I must have a talk to Matron—take steps to ensure that a situation like this doesn't happen again—we simply must make sure we have adequate trained staff.'

He moved away as Beth came back with a tea-tray, but turned at the door to say, 'Incidentally, mother and babe are doing well.' After a moment's hesitation, he added, 'Thanks to you.'

'I'm glad. How was the baby's Apgar at five minutes? I rated it at seven at one minute.'

The Apgar score was used to rate an infant's physical condition, with reference to its heart rate, respiratory effort, muscle tone, reflexes and colour, at one minute, then five, after delivery.

'It was up to ten at five minutes,' Dr Larsen said. 'Later on, when you're feeling like it, Louise can bring in the case-notes for you to write up.'

'I'll be glad to.'

He departed, and Sam, piling apricot jam and cream on to a scone, hoped that his more amiable frame of mind would last throughout the suturing of her leg, which, she feared, could take some time. But, for now, a cup of tea had never tasted so good.

The sister bustling about the small theatre where Sam's resuturing was to be done was unfamiliar to Sam. It would have been nice to have had Louise in attendance, but she was probably still busy in Maternity.

Gillian Marsh introduced herself to Sam. She was a tall, willowy brunette, with lots of self-confidence—probably one of the nurses on whom the hospital called when it needed extra staff, but not a midwife, or Louise would have called her in for the breech. Sam noticed she was not wearing a wedding-ring.

When Tony Larsen came in, it was immediately apparent that he and Gillian Marsh knew one another well—and got along just fine. With her, he was relaxed and affable, chatting away as he injected the local anaesthetic Gillian handed him and waited for it to take effect.

He gave Gillian a full account of the breech delivery and, to Sam's amazement, added a strong commendation of her handling of it. Wonders will never cease, she thought.

Gillian said, 'Indeed!' 'How nice!' a couple of times, in a voice that had cooled perceptibly, although the warmth was back again when, deftly changing the subject, she asked, 'And how is Bridie, Tony? How long has she to go now?'

'She's fine,' said Tony enthusiastically. 'Her EDC is mid-June—about three months.'

So Tony Larsen was married. And very much so, apparently, with a pregnant wife.

Sam felt herself plummet into another of the bouts of
depression that had been plaguing her since the accident.
She lost interest in what the other two were saying, and
lay watching, without much interest, Tony's long gloved
fingers putting tiny stitches in her right thigh. Judging
by the size of the laceration, she must have come into
contact with a fair-sized slab of broken glass in the bus.
Fortunately, only the lower part of the wound had
opened up as a result of her bumping it in the labour
ward.

When she began listening again, Gillian and Tony
Larsen were discussing a barbecue which was to be held
at Tony's property in something over a week's time.
Names were passed back and forth. It was clearly going
to be a big party—a bit much for a doctor's wife in her
third trimester of pregnancy to cope with, Sam thought.
But then country women were known to be capable.

Was she beautiful, Sam wondered, this wife of Tony
Larsen? Was she dark or fair? Tall or petite? What kind
of a baby would they have?

Sam winced.

The doctor paused. 'Sorry—did that hurt? Do you
need more LA?'

'No,' she insisted quickly. 'I can't feel anything,
really.'

'Sure? Sing out if you do.'

As he resumed his stitching, he began talking to Sam
now, asking her about her travels around Australia, her
impressions of this place and that, her plans for the
remainder of her time Down Under.

For once he was behaving like a human being towards
her. She liked that, very much indeed, and had hastily
to remind herself how objectionable he could be in a
different sort of mood, and how he had taken an instant
dislike to her, as, indeed, she had to him. Which was as
well, because, if it had been otherwise, the news that he

was married would have come as a shock, to say the least. Whereas now. . .

She stifled a sigh and closed her eyes, wishing it was all over.

His glance shifted from her thigh to her face. She looked very pale, very lovely, her long lashes dark against her cheeks. That was how he had first seen her, and, hard as he had tried since then to get her out of his mind, he hadn't been able to do so. In fact, he was feeling now just as he had felt then: smitten, somehow—confused—deeply dissatisfied with life—wanting more but knowing it was out of reach.

To hide a sudden tremulousness in his hands, one of which was holding a pair of Mosquito forceps and the other a fine Gillies needle-holder-cum-scissors, he stood erect and stretched, muttering something about its being a long job.

Immediately Samantha's eyes flew open—those incredibly large blue eyes—and met and held his. He wished he could read her thoughts in their depths, and heard himself ask, 'What have you been thinking about, lying there?'

'Oh, you know. . .we philosophical English. . . I was just thinking that it's true what they say, that forbidden fruit is sweet.' He could have no possible idea what she was talking about, she thought.

He looked startled.

'What inspired you to think that? What forbidden fruit did you have in mind?'

She couldn't tell him that, so she prevaricated. 'Before this happened today, I was hoping to get back to work soon. Now, knowing that I won't be able to for some time, I'm even more eager to do so.'

And that's the truth too, she thought. But only half of it.

'Oh yes, of course,' he said flatly, and bent his back to his task.

After a few minutes she asked, 'How long will it be?'

'Just a few minutes.'

'No, I meant how long until I can leave here?'

'A week at least.'

'And then I can travel?'

'I would expect so—with certain restrictions. And always supposing there are no further setbacks. Definitely no more escapades like this morning's. Though that's not quite the right word. . ."exploit" would be a better one, I guess.'

He smiled at her and the creases deepened in his cheeks. Sam wondered what it would be like to run her fingers down them. Damn! Had she no control over her thoughts these days?

She was sure of one thing—if she had to stay here for another week, she must see that she had plenty to occupy her mind. She would ask Louise to get her some books to read, she'd write lots of letters, plan her return to London, to work. . .

Anything, as long as she didn't have time to think about unpredictable hick doctors who treated one abominably one minute and had one's heart turning cartwheels the next, just because they happened to smile at you.

CHAPTER FIVE

TONY LARSEN made his usual early morning visit to the hospital next day.

He favoured Sam with an unsmiling 'Good morning', then said curtly to Sister Benson who accompanied him, 'Case-notes, please, Sister.'

Sister handed him the file and she and Sam watched as he took a pen from his pocket and wrote something on the notes. He held it out for Sister to read what he had written, and when she nodded, extended it in turn to Sam. Sam saw, in large letters, 'MINIMAL AMBULATION' and pulled a wry face.

'At least it's better than RIB, I guess,' she said.

'Only marginally. It means 'Shower only' for three days and, other than that, RIB. And I warn you,' he added grimly, 'any infringement will result in RIP. Is that understood?'

Sam nodded meekly. 'Yes, sir!' she said, and saw his features relax fractionally.

'We'd better keep her occupied, Sister. Can you rustle up a TV set?'

'Yes, I think we can manage that.'

'Right! Then I'll see you tomorrow.'

When he did appear next morning, he was carrying an armful of books which he deposited on Sam's overbed table, nodding approval, as he did so, at the television set at the end of her bed.

His visit was once again brief and, when he had gone, Sam sat forward and looked at the titles of the books, curious to see what he considered suitable reading for a young lady in her situation.

She chuckled. Clearly he had had difficulty deciding, so had brought a wide selection of titles. There was *Fever* by Robin Cook, clearly expected to appeal to her as a nurse, *Light a Penny Candle* by Maeve Binchy; Sam wondered whether his wife had had a hand in choosing that, but dismissed the idea when she saw that the next one was *The Hunt for Red October* by Tom Clancy—clearly a man's book and one which she did not think would appeal to her. As well, there were several paperbacks, mostly romances. They were all resting on a large glossy hardcover book, called *The Whitsundays*. Sam pulled it out and began leafing through it, then saw that there was an inscription on the fly-leaf. It read, 'Memories. With all my love, darling. Trish.'

Sam lay back against her pillows, turning the pages of the book and allowing her imagination to run riot. Before long, she felt she had all the ingredients for a romance novel of her own, with an eternal triangle comprising Tony, Trish and Bridie, playing out a steamy love story against a background of blue seas and skies, white sails and luxury pleasure resorts. Obviously, somewhere before the happy ending, Tony confessed to Bridie all about his affair with Trish, and was forgiven. How else was the book Trish had given him in memory of some magical interlude still to be found in his library?

Sam had already read *Fever*, as well as every word of every one of Maeve Binchy's books. She put them aside and arranged the remainder in a pile beside her, resolving to read the first few pages of each, before choosing the one which she found most gripping.

Unexpectedly, *Red October* won hands down, and she spent the rest of the day in a world of suspense and intrigue somewhere under the icy waters of the North Atlantic.

But it wasn't *Red October* she was reading when Tony Larsen walked through her door at his usual time next morning. It was *The Whitsundays*, and somehow, as she laid it on the bed, it happened to fall open at the fly-leaf.

She watched the doctor's face as he looked down at it, and saw his mouth tighten and two vertical lines appear between his dark eyebrows. He had probably forgotten all about that telltale inscription when he had selected the book to lend to her. But if Sam had hoped he would say something revealing she was disappointed. He picked the book up, snapped it shut, laid it on her table and asked, 'How's your leg?'

'Fine, thank you. . .When. . .?'

'We'll see. Perhaps tomorrow.'

And that, for today, was that.

Next day, Tony Larsen had Sister remove the dressings from Sam's wound. He appeared satisfied, even commended Sam on her good behaviour, and told Sister that, if she would kindly remove alternate sutures, Sam could be allowed up for a short time and could walk a short distance.

'Perhaps as far as the staff-room?' suggested Sister.

'Sounds reasonable.'

So Sam, with half the number of stitches in her wound and her leg freshly bandaged, spent almost an hour sitting in a comfortable chair in the staff-room, drinking coffee and chatting to the nurses as they dropped in in ones and twos for their morning break.

Much of the talk was about a barbecue that was shortly to be held. Sam pricked up her ears, realising that this must be what Tony Larsen and Gillian Marsh had been discussing in Theatre last week. She learned that it was the annual fund-raising event organised by the Ladies' Hospital Auxiliary, and that it was indeed to be held at the doctor's property. One year the ladies had staged a ball, last year a fête. Everyone seemed to think a barbecue would be the best yet.

Sam wondered, again, how a pregnant Bridie Larsen would cope with the crowd that was expected to attend, but nobody mentioned Bridie, and Sam didn't want to raise the subject herself. She did glean snippets of information about Tony Larsen. As she had suspected, he was a country farmer as well as a doctor, spending whatever time he could on his property a few miles out of town. He and his wife had come to Wirrando from New South Wales a couple of years ago and nobody knew much about them before that. Everybody knew that their marriage wasn't a happy one. It seemed his wife had never settled down to country life and spent most of her time in the city.

Everyone was invited to the barbecue, of course, although some would have to remain on duty. Sister Benson declared she was too old for such shindigs and would hold the fort, with one nurse, if someone would volunteer. Everyone volunteered, but Beth was the most persistent.

'I'm the logical one to stay,' she declared.

'That's nonsense. You'll go, my girl, if anyone does,' said Sister.

Sister's word was law, so that was that. The others decided they would draw lots that evening.

Later, when Sam was back in bed and Louise came to her room with a copy of *Woman's Weekly*, Sam asked what Beth had meant by saying that she was the logical one to stay behind on duty.

'Oh, Beth always thinks she's lowest one on the totem pole,' Louise explained.

'But why? She's not the most junior of the nurses, nor the worst by a long shot.'

'No, but she suffers from an innate sense of inferiority because of her colour.'

'That's deplorable! Does it really make any difference to anyone?'

'Only to Beth, but I don't think she broods about it—just accepts it as a fact of life.'

'Well, I'm very glad Sister Benson insisted that she go to the barbecue.'

'So are we all.'

Louise stood up. Then she paused, looking thoughtful, and sat down again.

'Sam,' she said, 'why don't you come too?'

'Come where?'

'To the barbecue, of course.'

'But I haven't been invited.'

'It's open house. As long as you pay your twenty dollars for the hospital fund you're welcome.'

'But it would mean staying on after I've been discharged.'

'Only for a day or two. And it *would* be fun.'

Already Sam's doubts were giving way before the realisation of how much, how very much, she wanted to meet Tony Larsen socially. So far, he had seen her in nothing more glamorous than nightgowns borrowed from Louise or her old blue dressing-gown. If she could, just once, meet him on his own level and not as doctor and patient!

Already her mind was leaping ahead, wondering what she could wear. Her wardrobe consisted mainly of jeans and T-shirts—ideal for trekking round Australia but not exactly designed to wow a country doctor. Then, with bubbling excitement, she remembered the dress she had bought in Hong Kong to wear at the Adelaide Festival of Arts Fringe concert. Like the Festival Fringe, it was slightly outrageous, a draped, vividly-coloured creation with a sash of some golden stuff—definitely over the top for a country barbecue, but quite ideal for her purpose.

Thinking of the Festival Fringe reminded her of Michael—Michael Platt, who was coming to Adelaide with a band, from London, to play in a Fringe concert.

She had promised to meet him there, if her itinerary made it at all possible. Michael, on somewhat flimsy grounds, considered himself her boyfriend, but for reasons she couldn't quite define, Sam knew that state of affairs couldn't be allowed to continue.

But the immediate thing was to get to that barbecue!

'You've talked me into it,' she told Louise. 'But will you do me one favour? Please don't tell anyone I'm planning to go to the barbecue, least of all Tony Larsen. After all, it is going to be at his place, and I could hardly turn up there if, as my doctor, he advised against it—because of the state of my leg, or whatever.'

'But you're bound to be discharged before Friday. What will you do in the meantime?'

'It would only be a couple of days at most. I'll go to the motel and lie low and not tell a soul I'm still around town.'

In case Louise was beginning to wonder why she was waxing so enthusiastic about the prospect of the barbecue, she said heartily, 'I've always wanted to go to a real Aussie bush barbie. It will be a marvellous grand finale to my stay here.'

Louise laughed. 'You came in with a bang—you might as well go out with one.'

'And you won't breathe a word to anyone?'

'On my honour!'

'You're a real pal.'

'"Mate" is the word Down Under, pal, especially at a barbie.'

On Tuesday morning, Tony Larsen arrived early at the hospital to officially discharge Samantha Hayes. It was not a duty he was looking forward to, and any faint subconscious hope he might have cherished that she would be reluctant to leave took wing when he saw her.

She had a sparkle in her eyes and colour in her cheeks,

and was quite obviously thrilled to be going. Her hair was still damp from her shower and curled about her face, which was innocent of make-up but none the less appealing for that. She looked very young and very lovely as she smiled up at him and said, 'Hello, Doctor!'

'Hi! So today's the big day,' he said tritely.

'Uh-huh!'

'Are all your arrangements in order?'

'Yes. Louise has looked after everything for me at this end.'

'And when you reach Adelaide?'

'I'm spending a few days with Eleanor Purvis—they were most insistent that I do that. Then I plan to fly back to England and find myself a job.'

England! The other side of the globe! And there wasn't a thing he could do to stop her. And this, he thought wryly, from a guy who a week ago was pushing for her immediate discharge so that he could get her out of his life!

All he could think of to say now was, 'I'd better have a last look at that leg. Thank you, Sister.'

Sister Benson removed the used breakfast tray from Sam's overbed table, then unwound the bandage from her leg. Tony Larsen probed gently and grunted approval.

'That shouldn't give you any more trouble. And otherwise? Physically? Emotionally? Are you sure you feel up to travelling?'

'I can honestly say I have no qualms at all about my immediate future. In fact, I'm looking forward to it with a great deal of interest.'

He could see that for himself. 'Then I can only wish you well,' he said, and held out his hand. She placed hers in it. It was a small, cool hand, and it grasped his firmly for a moment as she said, 'Thank you for everything.'

'My pleasure! Goodbye, then.'

'Au revoir.'

Au revoir! Till we meet again! Clearly, French wasn't her forte! He wished he could think it *was* just 'au revoir', but the chances of their meeting again were roughly one in a few million.

He repeated firmly, 'Goodbye,' and walked away.

He should have been glad to have seen the last of his troublesome patient, but next morning, when he did his rounds, the hospital seemed empty, even though he had a full list of patients to see. Somebody else, a middle-aged woman in for a gynae repair job tomorrow, was in Samantha's bed, and, although Tony was on friendly terms with her, this morning she seemed like an interloper.

That day and the next, the hospital staff, and indeed the whole town, were talking about the barbecue. Tony thought he must be the only one who was not looking forward to it, and wondered why he had ever allowed himself to be conned into having it at East Winds. It was a good thing Gillian had agreed to act as hostess for him. She was capable and charming, and, after Trish's phone call last night. . . His lips tightened.

On Friday he had his usual early morning gallop, showered, supervised the unloading of a truckful of trestle-tables and chairs and helped the men set them up under the trees. After that, he thankfully handed the house over to a swarm of auxiliary ladies and went off, to spend the day in the hospital and his consulting-rooms, returning home only in time to shower again and dress. Then, with Gillian beside him, he went out to greet the first of the guests.

It was a lovely evening after a moderately hot day. With daylight saving, it was not yet dark, but the lights slung between the trees had been turned on and added a fairytale touch to the scene. A slight breeze stirred the leaves of the gum trees and rustled the crisp white paper which covered the long tables. Smoke was beginning to rise from the barbecue area. Auxiliary ladies were handing drinks to guests as they arrived.

Tony, dressed in dark trousers and a pale khaki open-neck shirt, knew he should be feeling festive, but, in spite of Gillian, svelte and charming and very much at ease at his side, he felt restless and bored and lonely. Lonely? In the middle of a crowd like this? He frowned and made a quick impatient movement of his hand. Gillian, aware, turned and smiled at him encouragingly.

'Try and forget it,' she said.

She was referring to Trish's phone call, which he had told her about earlier this evening. But he hadn't been thinking about that—not for some time, anyway.

He continued to smile, say 'Hello', shake hands, kiss cheeks, and chat with people, occasionally parrying a question from someone who was seeking free medical advice. He was used to that—it was an occupational hazard.

The crowd grew. Everyone in town must be here by now. The mouthwatering aroma of grilling meat began to waft over from the barbecue.

Tony said, 'Enjoy yourselves,' to an elderly couple, and turned to greet his next guests. Louise, from the hospital, and with her. . . He looked again. It couldn't be! Samantha Hayes! She was looking incredibly lovely and smiling at him, tentatively, as if not quite sure of her welcome.

He found his voice with difficulty.

'Well! You're the very last person I expected to find here! Have you had a relapse or something?' He couldn't quite keep a note of hope out of his voice.

'Definitely not. I just decided to stay round for a while longer.'

'And you're really feeling all right? No more problems?'

'No, and, even if I had, I wouldn't want to discuss them here. This is a social occasion, after all.'

He laughed. 'I wish all my patients thought like that!'

She laughed too, and suddenly they were all talking, easily, happily. All but Gillian, who had become silent. When Tony said to Sam, 'Seeing this is a social occasion, you'll have to call me Tony,' Gillian said shortly, 'Everyone seems to be here now, Tony. I'll leave you to it,' and walked away.

Tony called after her, somewhat vaguely, 'Yes, of course. Thanks for your help, Gill.'

He spoke to the two girls standing with him, but his eyes were on Samantha as he said, 'You're both looking very nice tonight.'

Louise laughed. 'It sure beats uniform!'

'Or nightgowns,' said Sam. 'Not that your nightgowns weren't lovely, Louise.' They all laughed again.

Louise was wearing wide black silk trousers and a vivid blue silk top. Samantha had added gold sandals to her Hong Kong outfit. Tony caught himself wondering whether he could encircle that tiny waist with his hands, and said hastily, 'You've got more colour in your cheeks than you had.'

'I've been down on the beach for an hour or two each day, with Louise's help.'

'Why do I have the feeling it was you who put her up to this?' he said to Louise, and had to resist an urge to hug her.

'Guilty,' admitted Louise cheerfully. 'But she didn't need much persuading.'

Tony found that interesting. 'But I was under the impression that you were keen to get back to work?' he quizzed Sam.

'Yes, I am. But I found I couldn't pass up the chance to attend a real Aussie barbecue before I left.'

So put that in your pipe and smoke it, Tony Larsen, he told himself.

'Then we'd better see what the barbie's got to offer!'

He placed himself between the two girls and they moved off towards the tables. Sam was acutely aware of him, so close to her. As she stepped from the path on to the lawn, his hand grasped her arm to steady her, and he did not take it away until they stopped beside the tables.

As she stood there with Tony, helping themselves from the huge bowls of salads, baskets of crisp bread rolls and platters of grilled steaks, sausages and kebabs, the pain and depression of the past week or so seemed to Sam a distant memory.

She was sure Tony had been glad to see her. She had seen it in his eyes, and, just for a moment and quickly suppressed, there had been something else there too—something she couldn't quite define, but which had made her heart beat more rapidly for a while. She wished she knew him well enough to be able to read him better.

Before long Tony was drawn into another group of guests, and Sam took the opportunity to ask Louise, 'Is Tony's wife here?'

Louise shook her head. 'Not likely, with Gillian playing hostess. I'd have been surprised if she *had* put in an appearance.'

Why was that? Because she was pregnant—perhaps not feeling well? Or because of their marriage problems? Sam didn't have the chance to ask Louise more just then, as they were discovered by a group of nurses, all surprised to see Sam. There were bursts of laughter as they were told the story of her lying low for two days, and the reason for it, according to Louise.

Beth was there, hand in hand with a shy, nice-looking youth who obviously had eyes for no one else. Sam gathered that this was a new development and that everyone was delighted for Beth.

When the guests had finished eating and the tables were cleared away, people began dancing to the music relayed through speakers attached to the eaves of the house.

Every now and again Sam found Tony Larsen at her side. He didn't ask her to dance, obviously because of her leg. But, every time he was there, she experienced a feeling of contentment, of tranquillity almost. This, she thought, is all I can take with me when I go back to England—a memory. But a memory she would treasure for the rest of her life. If she hadn't come tonight, she wouldn't have had even that.

Towards the end of the evening, Sam left the party and made her way into the house. She found the bathroom and freshened up, then walked back slowly.

It was a large, sprawling house, single-storeyed and comfortable. She peeped into a big sitting-room and then into a small library or den which was clearly a male preserve and therefore must be Tony's. It was illuminated only by the light from a small chandelier in the hallway, but she could see bookcases lining the walls, a desk and a couple of big leather chairs.

She realised how tired she felt and that the ache in her leg was growing worse. She hesitated only a moment before going into the room and sitting down in one of the chairs. It was deep and comfortable, and she breathed a sigh of relief and closed her eyes.

Her respite was short-lived. So short-lived, in fact, that when she heard Tony Larsen's voice she wondered whether he had followed her here.

'Tired?' he asked.

'A little. I hope you don't mind—it looked so inviting.'

'Has tonight been too much for you?' he asked.

'No. I've enjoyed every minute.'

'Can I get you anything? A drink?'

'No, thank you. I've done more than well already. If this is a typical Aussie barbecue, I'm impressed.'

'The ladies from the Auxiliary do a marvellous job.'

It was all very formal, very conventional. But the sense of serenity was there again, and, as Tony sat down in the chair opposite, she knew that he felt it too. She had never seen him so relaxed, so free of the tenseness she had come to associate with him, and of the hostility he had so often manifested towards herself.

Neither of them spoke for several minutes, then he stirred restlessly and, even in the dim light, Sam could see the brooding sadness in his face again. It was not to be wondered at. He looked, in fact, as any man would look who had had to host a major social function without his wife at his side. Or a man whose first child was expected in a matter of weeks, but whose wife chose to spend most of her time away from him. Sam tried to imagine what problems that would pose after the child was born.

Tony stirred first. 'Well, I must do my duty by my guests, I suppose. Do stay and keep off that leg for as long as you wish. I'll tell Louise where to find you when she's ready to go home.'

'Thanks, but I think I'll go back too.'

They both stood up at the same instant and it was as though an electric current arced across the space that separated them. Sam couldn't have said, afterwards, who had moved first, but she was in his arms and he was kissing her, hungrily, urgently.

It was totally unexpected, but she knew instantly that all evening she had been wanting it to happen. She allowed her body to melt against his and respond in a rising, irresistible tide of passion.

Minutes passed before she was able to clutch at the
fleeting remnants of common sense. This man, in whose
arms she was and in whose arms she so desperately
wanted to remain, was not only married but his wife was
expecting his baby. Moreover, he had made it plain
beyond doubting that he didn't even like Sam. So these
passionate kisses were just that. . .passion. It was a word
that embraced several things—his anger against his wife,
perhaps a few too many drinks with his guests, and, of
course, proximity.

As all this flashed through Sam's mind, she found the
strength to turn her head away and groan a desperate,
'No!' Tony became very still and did not try to kiss her
again, but his arms still held her so tightly she could
scarcely breathe.

'Please!' she gasped, 'please!' and arched her body,
straining away from him.

He released her slowly and they moved apart. But the
fire was still there and, in spite of everything her mind
had told her, she wanted nothing more in this world
than to be in his arms again. If he had made the slightest
movement towards her she would not have been able to
resist.

But the only movement he made was to draw back,
saying stiffly, 'I'm very sorry. I hadn't intended that to
happen.'

'Nor had I.' Intended, no. Wanted, yes, yes, yes!

They were both silent for a space, before Sam, in an
effort to get back to reality, said, 'Your wife's not here
tonight?'

He replied shortly, 'No.'

'Is she keeping well?'

'As far as I know. Why do you ask?' He sounded
surprised, angry even, that she should have mentioned
his wife.

'I thought she might not have felt able to cope with a big party. I understand she's pregnant.'

'Pregnant? Where on *earth* did you get that idea?' He was so obviously dumbfounded that Sam had a horrible feeling she had put her foot in it again.

'I heard you and Gillian Marsh talking—in Theatre, while you were stitching up my leg. She asked how Bridie was and you talked about her EDC.'

Unexpectedly, Tony gave vent to a gust of laughter. 'Bridie!' he spluttered.

'I don't understand. Unless. . . Bridie is. . .someone else. . .not your wife?'

'Such as some woman I keep tucked away—a mistress?'

Sam protested, 'I didn't mean that!'

'Just to put the record straight, I don't have a mistress, my wife's name is Trish, and the very last thing she would want to be is pregnant.' His lips twisted in a bitter smile. 'I'd better qualify that—to be pregnant *by me* is about the very last thing she'd want to be.'

He turned to her and held out his hand.

'Come with me,' he said.

Sam hesitated, fearful of further physical contact with him. But the tension between them had been broken and she was able, at least to all outward appearances, to place her hand in his quite naturally, and allow herself to be led out of the room.

Mystified, she went with him along a passage, through a large kitchen and out through a back door. From here, the sounds of the party were muted, but it was obviously still in full swing. It seemed like an eternity since Tony had found her in the library, but, in reality, was probably no more than ten minutes.

At the back of the house, extending out from the veranda that encircled the entire house, was a brick-paved patio with huge ferns and numerous plants in

terracotta pots among some well-used cane chairs.
Beyond the patio was a grassed area bounded by a
white-railed fence.

Tony stopped at the fence and called softly, 'Bridie!
Bridie!'

A gentle whinny answered him and the sounds of
hoofs on turf, before a horse emerged from a clump of
trees across the paddock and trotted towards them. It
was a palomino mare, her flowing mane and tail gleaming white in the moonlight.

'Oh, she's beautiful!' breathed Sam. 'May I pat her?'

'Of course. She's my pride and joy. And, as you can
see, she's quite pregnant.'

Sam laughed ruefully. 'I feel very foolish. It just goes
to show one shouldn't listen to gossip.'

'And that doctors shouldn't gossip in their patients'
hearing,' added Tony. With his hand caressing the
horse's neck, he added, 'You probably won't be able to
avoid hearing gossip about my wife and me before
long—if you haven't already?' He looked at her with
raised eyebrows.

'I've heard that your marriage isn't entirely happy,'
Sam replied frankly.

'Everyone knows that, I guess. What they don't know
is that Trish has started divorce proceedings. I was only
told, by phone, a couple of nights ago.'

And hence, thought Sam, the bitterness, the pent-up
anger, the passionate kiss in the library a short time ago.

'I'm sorry,' she said.

'Thanks. I am too, but it had to come—just a matter
of time, really.' The lightness in his voice was forced.

She waited for him to continue, but all he said was, 'I
must get back to the party. Some people might be
wanting to leave early.'

But he seemed reluctant to go. Sam too wanted to
prolong this moment, in the moonlight, with music in

the background, and the beautiful animal. . . She wished that. . .kiss in the library had never happened.

Tony must have been thinking the same thing.

'Can you forget what happened earlier?' he asked her suddenly.

She could just see his face, the strong angle of his jaw, the line of his hair against his neck.

'No,' she said, 'I don't think I can forget it. But I know better than to attach any significance to it.'

'Put it down to proximity, eh?'

'Something like that.'

'Powerful stuff, proximity!' Sam knew, by the bitterness in his voice, that he was thinking about his marriage, with its notable lack of proximity.

To change the subject she said, 'I've had my wish and seen an Aussie barbecue. It's been quite an experience. I want to thank you.'

'And now you'll be going home.'

'Yes.'

They began to move back towards the house.

'When do you plan to leave?' Tony asked.

'I haven't made any reservations yet—probably the day after tomorrow.'

He stopped as they reached the door off the patio, and, turning towards her, took her face gently between his hands and kissed her, just once, very lightly, on the lips.

'That's for goodbye,' he said.

'Goodbye,' she said, and looked down quickly so that he couldn't see that her eyes had filled with tears.

'If you don't mind,' she said, 'I'll wait here for Louise. If you see her, tell her where I am, please, and that there's no hurry.'

He nodded, turned and disappeared into the house. Sam sank into one of the chairs set among plants in a shaded corner of the patio.

It was almost ten minutes before Louise came looking for her, and Sam spent that time trying to marshal her fragmented thoughts into some sort of order.

She wasn't sure now whether she was glad she had come to the barbecue or not. Certainly the night had turned out to be wildly different from anything she had expected. What had it all meant? In spite of her light assurances to Tony, and her own rationalising of the incident, that kiss in the library had stirred her deeply. Then there was the knowledge that he was soon to be divorced.

And, last of all, and perhaps the most disturbing, his second kiss. She found it hard, impossible really, to put that down to some sudden impulse. It had been considered, deliberate, tender. And quite final.

She was glad she hadn't gone back to the party. She would have found it impossible to laugh and smile and behave as though nothing had happened. And she would have had to say goodbye to Tony again, with other people watching.

No—all she wanted, now, was to creep away quietly, and carry with her, in a small, warm place in her heart, the memory of his final kiss.

CHAPTER SIX

LOUISE came to the motel the following afternoon. She was still in uniform and agog with curiosity.

Sam had her suitcase open on the bed and most of her gear already packed in it. She was carefully folding her Hong Kong dress and thinking that she would never wear it in the future without bitter-sweet memories of last night, when she heard the knock on her door.

Louise didn't stand on ceremony. 'Sam, Matron wants to see you. Do come at once!'

Sam raised her eyebrows. That didn't sound like Matron, who usually couched her orders in much more diplomatic terms. As Sam stood up and reached for her hairbrush, she quizzed Louise, 'Did Matron really say to come at once?'

'No,' admitted Louise. 'She said "at your convenience". But I can't bear the suspense much longer. Tony Larsen has been in with her, having a long chat, and it must have been about you, and I'm dying to know——'

Sam interrupted the flow. 'Is Tony still there?' she asked.

'He's in the small theatre now, removing some skin cancers.'

'Some skin cancers could mean two or a dozen, so Tony could be tied up in Theatre for a short time or a long time. With a bit of luck, Sam would be able to have her talk with Matron and be out of the hospital again before he was free. She picked up her room key and dropped it in her bag. 'I'm as curious as you are now, so let's go.'

73

Matron smiled when she saw Sam, motioned her to sit down and came straight to the point.

'Do you have a permit to work in Australia, Samantha?'

So that was it! Work! Sam felt a stirring of excitement.

'Yes. I applied for one—just in case. But it's for three months only.'

'Right! If you didn't have one, that would be that.' There was a quick knock on the door and Matron called, 'Come in, Tony.' Clearly Tony was expected. He entered, still wearing a theatre gown and plucking at the strings of the mask which hung about his neck.

'Hello, there!' He smiled broadly at Sam. Last night might never have happened, she thought, not knowing whether to be relieved or disappointed. She smiled back.

'How far have you got?' Tony asked Matron eagerly.

'She has a work permit for three months.'

'Great! Carry on!' He pushed a chair so that he could see both Matron and Sam and sat down, stretching his long legs in front of him.

Matron spoke to Sam again. 'Several things recently have highlighted our need to do something about our staff shortage. First there was the bus accident, which really stretched us to the limit, and then you, a patient, had to help out in Maternity.' Matron pursed her lips and gave a small shudder. 'It's occurred to us that, if you don't have any firm plans for the immediate future, you might be willing to stand in the breach once again.'

Tony laughed suddenly and Matron paused, looking puzzled. Then she smiled. 'No pun intended,' she said, and went on, 'Finding extra permanent staff always takes time in a country hospital. If you could stay for the three months your permit allows it would be a tremendous help to us. Now, my dear, I know this has come as a surprise to you. You must take whatever time you need to think about it.'

Sam repressed a grin. Judging by the eager expressions on the faces of both Matron and Tony, who was leaning forward expectantly, they were prepared to allow her all of two minutes to make up her mind. She lowered her eyes, not so much to give herself time to think as to hide the fact that her initial reaction to their proposal was something akin to wild joy.

She didn't need even two minutes to consider. She knew she was going to stay, and she knew why. In two words, Tony Larsen!

She knew, even more clearly, that she would probably live to regret it. For starters, did she really want to spend three months working for a man she knew to be moody and temperamental, one who, moreover, had shown from the beginning of their acquaintance that he did not particularly like her? Last night had encouraged her to dare to hope he was beginning to change his mind about that. But, even so, he was in the process of being divorced, and the fact that he was patently unhappy about it must prove that he was still in love with his wife. By the end of three months they would probably be reconciled and she'd have wasted three months of her life living in cloud-cuckoo land.

So what? All her pros and cons were irrelevant. She simply couldn't go, not while there was the slenderest ray of hope to hold on to.

She looked up, ready to tell them she had made up her mind, but Tony forestalled her.

'I should have explained more fully what we have in mind, if you do stay. Do you type?'

Sam was not too surprised by the question, assuming that they would want her to assist in the office when she was not needed on the wards. 'I used to,' she said. 'I haven't done so for some time, but I'm sure I could manage office typing.'

Tony made a dismissive gesture. 'It's more interesting

than that,' he said. 'I've been working on a research project for some time and have been very frustrated that I can't find more time to spend on it. There's still a lot of work to be done, but it would help tremendously, at this juncture, if I had someone who could type up my rough notes so I could then revise and edit them.'

So there it was! Tony's reason for wanting her to stay. She could tell by the eagerness in his voice that his research project meant more to him even than the welfare of the hospital. It meant so much, in fact, that he was prepared to put up with her presence for three months to see it progressing. Well, she hadn't yet said she would stay. She could still opt out.

He went on explaining. 'I have a word processor, but even so, it won't be an easy job. The notes are very rough and I'm a lousy writer.'

Sam smiled. 'What doctor isn't?'

He acknowledged the truth of that with a cheerful shrug. 'Someone who understands medical jargon would have a head start deciphering it. How do you feel about having a go?'

'Sounds fun. What's the research about?'

'The cardiological effects of drugs of addiction. I began it while we. . .while I was still in the city. Since coming here, I've expanded it to include the effects of alcohol on Aborigines—for obvious reasons.'

Sam nodded her understanding. 'Would you spell out just what you would expect me to do?'

'We're suggesting, really, that you float between the hospital and my rooms, where my computer is set up. When you're not needed at the hospital, you could put in as many hours as you feel able working on the project. My receptionist, Helen, works from eleven to four most days. She types accounts, but she's not a nurse and, as I said, a nurse would have a decided advantage working on the project.'

Sam turned to Matron. 'And where would I live?'

'There's room in the nurses' quarters,' Matron told her.

They were both looking at her, eager to know her decision. She had prevaricated long enough. 'I would like to stay,' she said.

Tony leaped to his feet. 'Great! I'll hunt out the first pages of my notes so you can get started tomorrow. That is, of course,' he added as an afterthought, 'if you're feeling up to it.'

'Tomorrow is Sunday,' Matron reminded him. 'Samantha might like a day to shift and settle in.'

His face fell, until Sam said, 'I'm almost packed already. I'd be happy to start tomorrow.'

'Good girl! Ten o'clock? In my rooms?'

'Yes.'

As Sam left Matron's office she was waylaid by Louise, who must have been lurking for just that purpose. Sam, feeling more than a little bemused by the unexpected change in her plans for the future, told Louise what had transpired. Louise was delighted, and typically, took charge.

'I'll go back to the motel with you now and help you move into the home. And you'll need uniforms, and more clothes. I'm off on Monday, so we could go into Lincoln and have a shopping spree.'

At ten o'clock next morning, Sam was in Tony Larsen's consulting-rooms, wondering which would prove to be her biggest bugbear, the word processor in front of her, challenging her to master its complexities, or the untidy pile of notepaper on the table beside it, covered with masses of indecipherable hieroglyphics.

Tony laughed at the look of dismay on her face.

'I did warn you! If you want to change your mind. . .?'

'Never!' said Sam stoutly. 'Do you have an instruction manual for this monster?'

'Yes. But if I show you that you probably *will* walk out. I'll get you set up so all you need do is key the stuff in, quite roughly. By the time we get around to editing, you'll have developed some degree of rapport with this baby.' He patted the machine lovingly. 'Sit down and I'll show you the basics.'

He placed a chair for her in front of the keyboard, then sat beside her, resting an arm along the back of her chair as he slipped a disk into the machine, waited for it to stop whirring and then tapped keys which brought up words on the screen.

Sam tried to concentrate on the words, but they were double Dutch to her, and she was sure she would never be able to learn anything with him so close to her that his hand brushed hers occasionally. She dropped both her hands into her lap and tried to look intelligent as she gazed at the screen.

Gradually her agitation subsided and she became interested in what he was doing. He stayed for half an hour, and by the time he left, saying he would be at home if she needed him for anything, she felt confident she could begin keying in his notes.

When he had gone, she looked around her curiously. So this was where he spent much of his time—where he saw his patients. She was in a large reception-room which had been partitioned off in one corner by a right-angled, two-tiered counter to make an office area. As well as her computer there were a rather more anti-quated typewriter, a telephone, numerous pigeonholes containing forms and stationery, several large books and, against the wall, two cabinets of files, obviously used for case-notes.

Sam was tempted to explore the rest of the suite of rooms, but decided to remain at the computer and apply what Tony had told her, while it was still fresh in her mind. She read through a page or two of his notes, trying to familiarise herself with his handwriting. As he had said, it was atrocious, even for a doctor, but it was his, and therefore she found it, as well as the substance of his text, absorbing. She touched a key tentatively, then another, and felt absurdly excited to see words pop up on the screen.

An hour later she was completely absorbed, so much so that when the phone rang near her elbow she jumped. That would be Tony, ringing to see how she was getting on. But it was a woman's voice that responded to Sam's 'Hello,' a distraught woman's voice, demanding to speak to the doctor.

'I'm sorry, Doctor's not here at the moment. This is Sister speaking. May I help you?' asked Sam.

'It's my husband—I think he's having a heart attack!'

'Your name is Mrs. . .'

'Whittaker. What shall I do, Sister?'

'How bad is he?'

Her chair was on wheels, and as she continued talking to Mrs Whittaker she propelled herself the few feet across to the filing cabinet, pulled open the drawer labelled S-W and, cradling the receiver on her shoulder, began flicking through the case-notes in the drawer.

'He's bad—he's hurting real bad!'

'Just where is the pain?'

'He says it's everywhere—in his chest and arms. He didn't feel very well early this morning, but he went back to bed and went to sleep, and then the pain woke him up.'

'Is he having trouble breathing?'

'Yes. And he says he feels sick and dizzy.'

'Is his name Theodore?'

'Yes, that's right. What will I do, Sister, please?'

Sam extracted a file from the drawer, and as she

pushed herself back to the counter she heard a key in the
door behind her, and turned to see Tony entering. She
beckoned to him and he came across and stood behind
her. As she continued talking to the distraught woman
on the other end of the line, she pointed a finger at the
name on the outside of the case-note folder, then wrote
MI in large letters on a pad on the counter. Tony took
the pencil from her, scrawled, 'On my way—ten minutes—call ambulance' and was out of the door at a run.

'Mrs Whittaker,' Sam said, 'prop your husband up on
two or three pillows and make him as comfortable as
you can. Tell him the doctor is on his way already and
that everything's going to be OK. Doctor will be there
in less than ten minutes.'

'Oh, thank you, Sister!' Mrs Whittaker's relief was
evident in her voice.

'I'm going to hang up now so that I can call an
ambulance, because Doctor will want to take your
husband into hospital, where he'll get the very best of
care.'

Sam pushed the button to disconnect the call and
immediately dialled again, first the ambulance, then the
hospital, alerting the staff to the imminent arrival of a
patient in coronary crisis. Matron answered the phone,
listened to what Sam had to say, then asked, 'Where are
you now?'

'In Dr Larsen's rooms.'

'Can you come to the hospital?'

'Of course.'

'I'll send a car.'

Sam pushed the scattered sheets of Tony's notes
together, deciding to leave the computer switched on
rather than attempt the unfamiliar exit process Tony
had explained she should follow when she had completed
her typing for the day. She grabbed her handbag, pulled
the door to behind her and was waiting on the footpath

when a car pulled in, with one of the hospital's two male nurses at the wheel. In three minutes she was at the hospital.

A hovering nurse told her to go straight to the intensive care unit—Matron's orders. She had time to check out the emergency equipment and to give herself a quick orientation course in the layout of the unit before she heard the ambulance arriving. She went out to meet it and, as the officers began pulling out the stretcher bearing the patient, she saw Tony's car pull in behind the ambulance and Tony and an elderly woman alight from it.

Tony raised his eyebrows when he saw Sam there, and asked, as they walked into the hospital behind the stretcher, 'Was this Matron's idea or yours?'

'Matron's.'

'Glad she thought of it.'

Matron appeared and took Mrs Whittaker under her wing, suggesting that she go into the visitors' lounge for a cup of tea while Mr Whittaker was being settled into bed.

Once the little procession reached the unit, Tony and Sam were fully occupied, seeing the patient transferred to bed, connecting him to a monitor for a twelve-lead ECG, and to the oxygen supply through a nasal cannula, replacing the mask which the ambulance officers had used. Tony informed Sam and the other nurse on ICU duty that the patient had had morphine and was in less pain. All the same, Sam noted, his skin had a greyish tinge, and the fact that he was keeping his eyes determinedly closed showed he was apprehensive.

'Your diagnosis was spot on,' Tony told Sam as they stood staring at the ECG monitor. 'Those pathologic Q-waves and the ST segment and T-wave changes indicate a transmural infarction.' He grinned suddenly. 'I should

say it's a "Q-wave infarction", I guess. That seems to be
the preferred term these days.'

A medico who keeps up with his reading, thought
Sam.

'We'll run a full series of tests, of course,' Tony
continued. 'Complete blood count, cardiac enzymes,
arterial blood gases, serum electrolytes. . . Can I leave
you to collect the samples?'

'Of course.' Sam was already busy writing the tests he
had asked for on a pathology request form. As she
handed the form to him to sign, a deep voice spoke up
from the bed.

'Lot o' jargon! What's it all mean, Doc?'

Mr Whittaker had opened his eyes and was glowering
at Tony from under jutting grey eyebrows.

'They're just routine blood-tests we do on all our heart
patients,' Tony told him cheerfully. 'One of the blood
vessels leading to your heart has become blocked and
the muscle is protesting because it can't get its usual
supply of blood. That's what's been giving you the pain.
It's not a bad attack, as heart attacks go, but I want you
to stay very quiet for a few days.'

'Not much chance o' runnin' away tied up to this lot!'
Mr Whittaker grumbled. Very tentatively he looked
around at the machines to which he was connected, then
seemed to gain confidence.

'And who's gonna look after me bleedin' farm, mate,
while I'm lyin' in this bleedin' bed—tell me that?' he
asked.

'I'll have a chat to your wife and we'll fix up something—find a neighbour to help out, maybe. Will you
trust me on this one?'

Patient stared at doctor and doctor at patient, before
the patient said grudgingly, 'Guess I'll 'avter. But tell
'em don't forget to watch the sheep in the south paddock.
Not much feed there—bloomin' drought!'

'Will do. Now *you* do just what Sister tells you to. You'll be out of here and looking after things yourself all the sooner if you do.'

Mr Whittaker cast a sceptical look at Sam and seemed about to make some disparaging remark, but met her firm unblinking gaze and subsided with a derisive 'Huh!' He closed his eyes again, and Sam and Tony exchanged smiles. Clearly, their patient's bark was going to be worse than his bite.

Tony gave Sam one or two further orders, then drew her towards the door, out of earshot of the bed.

'I feel this is all a bit much for you,' he said, looking at her keenly. 'Are you really up to it?'

She smiled. 'So far, so good.'

'Leg's OK?'

'Not too bad, thanks.'

'I'll tell Matron you're not to work longer than four-hour shifts for this week.'

Sam opened her mouth to protest, but thought better of it. 'You're probably right,' she admitted. 'And it *is* nice to have someone make the decisions for you.'

She smiled up at him gratefully, and was surprised to see his expression become set and hard.

'Yes, well. . .' he said, and turned and walked back to the bed, where he stood for some time, looking at the monitor and then down at the patient. He reached a hand to check for jugular vein distension and grunted his satisfaction. 'You'll do fine, mate,' he reassured Mr Whittaker, who opened one eye, grunted and closed it again.

Back at the door, Tony stopped and, looking at some point beyond Sam's shoulder, said, 'Call me at once if you need me, Sister,' and departed.

Sam felt absurdly deflated. He had quite clearly considered her last remark lacked professionalism. Perhaps she *had* allowed the mild feeling of euphoria she had been feeling all morning to make her less than professional. But Dr Larsen needn't worry! She would never allow anything to blunt her clinical acumen or affect her work in any way.

She moved back into the room, picked up her stethoscope and began a routine assessment of Mr Whittaker's vital signs, putting everything else firmly out of her mind.

Tony, having gone to the visitors' lounge and talked for some minutes with Mrs Whittaker, returned to his car and slid behind the wheel. But instead of driving away he sat for several minutes, gazing straight ahead. An onlooker would have assumed, from his slight frown and intent gaze, that he was preoccupied with the problems of one of his patients. But, in fact, he was seeing only a pair of entrancing blue eyes and a dimple dancing beside alluring lips.

Had he been a deluded fool to discount the spell that Samantha Hayes had had him under ever since his first sight of her? Should he have listened to the small but persistent inner voice that had tried to tell him he was not acting purely in the interests of the hospital, nor even of his research project, in suggesting to Matron that she invite Samantha Hayes to join the staff?

He had told himself, and Matron, that she was a good nurse and would be an asset to the hospital. He was still sure of that, after the way she had handled that breech delivery, and then the cardiac patient this morning. But he admitted now that he had been engaging in a nice little exercise in rationalisation, motivated by his personal desires, in suggesting that she be asked to stay on.

Chances were, of course, that he was letting himself in for a big disappointment, because, as well as being beautiful and desirable, Samantha was young and free. She could go where she liked and do what she liked.

What did he, Tony Larsen, have to offer a girl like that? For starters, he was years older than she. And the last few years had left him morose and embittered, with nothing to look forward to except a divorce. Even when he was finally free of Trish, he couldn't possibly wish whatever would be left on a girl like Samantha, in the unlikely event that she was disposed to hang around Wirrando that long.

He couldn't really understand why she had agreed to stay on at all. Probably long before the three months were up she would have got bored silly and taken off again for more interesting pastures. Back to work in London, as she had said she wanted to do. She probably had a boyfriend waiting back there too, he told himself, with determined masochism.

So, he'd got himself into this situation. He'd just have to sit it out for as long as she was here. The best thing to do would be to see as little of her as possible. And when he *did* see her he would make sure he kept his feelings firmly under control. After all the experience he'd had doing just that over the last few years, he should have made a better fist of it than he had in the last few days.

Of course, he couldn't expect to avoid seeing Samantha absolutely. After all, she *was* nursing his patient, and working on his project. . .

As he turned the key in the ignition and put the car into drive, his frown had quite disappeared and he was whistling softly through his teeth.

CHAPTER SEVEN

FOR the next three days Sam worked a four-hour shift in ICU, and managed, also, to spend some time each day working on Tony's research project.

With Helen's help, she fathomed enough of the mysteries of the word processor to become enthusiastic about its labour-saving potential. But unravelling the complexities of Tony's manuscript was another thing altogether. Obviously, it was in its original form and had been heavily edited more than once, so that the pages consisted of a tangle of deletions, insertions, brackets, arrows and his own peculiar proof-reading signs.

She had expected to be able to ask him about problems she encountered when she saw him from time to time. But for three days he didn't come to his rooms while she was there, and when she saw him in ICU she was wary of asking him about problems relating to her typing, in case she met with another rebuff.

On the fourth morning, when she and Helen had puzzled for half an hour, with the help of a large medical dictionary, over one word which, Sam felt sure, would prove to be the Open Sesame to a whole paragraph, she picked up the phone in utter frustration and dialled Tony's home number, where, he had told Helen, he would be at that time.

Sam half expected a rebuke, either for not being able to decipher his notes or for phoning him at home on other than a medical matter—or for both reasons.

But he replied affably when she said, 'It's Samantha here,' and listened patiently as she read out to him as much of the context of the problem word as she had been able to decipher. After a moment's thought, he told her the word she was wanting was 'Wenckebach' and went on to explain that that was a form of second-degree AV block.

Rather than risk spoiling his current amiability, she refrained from telling him that she knew all about the 'footsteps of Wenckebach' or that he had abbreviated the word in his notes beyond recognition. Instead, when he had finished, she said, 'Thank you. I'm sorry I had to bother you,' to which he replied, 'No trouble at all. I was hoping you might call. Any time.'

She hung up in a state of mind bordering on euphoria which, fortunately, Helen didn't notice, as the phone rang again and Helen became involved in a lengthy explanation to a patient about just when and how Doctor wanted her to take her medication.

But that afternoon, when Sam was on duty in ICU and Tony came in to see Mr Whittaker, his attitude was as formal and remote as it had ever been. Puzzled, Sam told herself he was worried about his patient, who was not making the progress they had all hoped he would. In fact, they were all concerned lest a second infarct should follow the first.

It transpired that Tony had decided not to dilly-dally any longer, but to transfer Mr Whittaker by ambulance to the city for more extensive tests.

'And what might they be?' Mr Whittaker demanded.

'I'm not a hundred per cent sure what they'll decide to do, but it will probably be something called "echocardiography,"' Tony told him.

'You doctors and your gobbledegook!' grumbled Mr Whittaker, and Tony went on, equably, to explain that during the test they'd bounce some ultrasound waves off his heart and that would give them a pretty fair idea what was going on in there.

'It's what they call a "non-invasive" test,' he said.

'You won't even have to have an injection, and it won't cause you any pain or pose any risk to you.'

Sam knew that Tony was purposely not mentioning other tests the doctors might decide to run, such as cardiac catheterisation and angiography, which could by no stretch of the imagination be called 'non-invasive'. Mr Whittaker was apprehensive enough already, and it would not help his condition to have him worrying about procedures which might never happen.

Tony said he'd arranged for the air ambulance for next morning. 'Have him ready by nine o'clock, please, Sister,' he ordered brusquely, and strode out.

Sam could have told him she would not be on duty at nine o'clock next morning, but, feeling dispirited and heavy, she wrote the order in the case-notes and repeated it to the nurse who took over from her later on.

With Mr Whittaker's transfer, Sam's time in ICU had come to an end. She was sorry about that, and not only because she had grown fond of the gruff old man and his long-suffering wife, who spent hours sitting by her husband, knitting and saying very little. Sam had come to look forward to the daily contact with Tony in ICU, even though he was often churlish and unpredictable.

She could, of course, be called on to help out in the hospital again soon, she realised, and brightened at the thought. Several of the staff were down with flu. Two nurses had already been off for three days and more were bound to follow. In the meantime, she could spend all day working on Tony's project. And, naturally, he would be in and out of his consulting-rooms. . .

Next morning she was awakened by a nurse calling her to the phone in the staff lounge. It was Matron.

'Have you had experience in operating theatre, Sister?' Matron asked.

'I've not had post-graduate experience, Matron, but our OR training was very thorough.'

'We have a child in with a strangulated hernia which needs immediate surgery. Dr Welsh brought him in a short while ago. Dr Larsen will do the surgery and Dr Welsh the anaesthesia. Sister Benson has started setting up OR, but she's up to her ears in her own ward with nurses off sick, so the sooner you can get over here the better.'

'Ten minutes, Matron.'

'Good girl!'

Sam had long ago done her own time-and-motion study on showering and dressing in the shortest possible time, and in slightly less than ten minutes she was speeding across the stretch of lawn which separated the home and the hospital. Both buildings were air-conditioned, and she was glad she didn't have to spend more than a minute or two getting from one to the other this morning. Although it was not much after seven, it was already oppressively hot and still, and there were heavy thunderheads building up over a leaden grey ocean.

In theatre, Sister Benson explained briefly what she had already done, and departed. Sam donned a gown, cap and mask and carried on where Sister had left off. Her scout nurse was busy with bowls and lotions, and Sam had time to look over the sterile instruments on the trolley and the array of needles and sutures Sister had selected.

Realising just how long it was since she had scrubbed for surgery, she began to wonder whether she had been over-confident in saying she could handle this. The butterflies in her stomach and her slightly accelerated heart-rate indicated that her adrenalin was flowing in response to the challenge. That wasn't a bad thing—as long as her hands were steady. She held them out in front of her and eyed them critically, then nodded, satisfied. Her scout nurse, Maisie Jenkins, caught her eye and grinned sympathetically.

Sam heard footsteps in the scrub-room and went out, to find Tony, in shirtsleeves, putting on a cap. As he reached for a mask, he said, 'So, here we are again? The ubiquitous Sister Hayes.'

Not sure what lay behind his comment, Sam bridled slightly and retorted, 'This *is* what you asked me to stay for, isn't it?'

He raised an eyebrow as he picked up a cake of soap and began to wash his hands. 'Of course! What else?'

There were sounds of movement in the theatre and Sam said, unnecessarily but in an attempt to calm her nerves, 'That must be the patient.'

'I haven't seen him yet,' commented Tony as he dried his hands. 'Charles made the diagnosis. I'll examine him, of course, before I start,' he added, to explain why he was not doing a proper scrub at this stage.

She followed him as he walked through into the theatre. A nurse, with her back to them, was laying a small form on the operating table. As she stepped aside, Tony moved forward. Sam moved too, to the other side of the table, carefully avoiding sterile trolleys as she went, and drew up the hospital gown the child was wearing, to allow Tony to begin his examination.

But he made no move to do so. Sam, looking up, was startled to see that his face, or as much of it as she could see for the mask, had turned quite white. His eyes were fixed on the face of the child on the table and, Sam thought, they looked quite. . .devastated.

Hadn't he been expecting the patient to be a child? Didn't he like operating on small children? She had known one surgeon in the past whose dislike of operating on children had amounted to a phobia, so much so that he had ultimately restricted his surgery to gynaecological patients only.

But Tony couldn't opt out now. He *had* to operate. There was no one else, and every minute with a strangulated hernia was important. To give him a chance to snap out of whatever was bugging him, she spoke to Charles Welsh, who was fiddling with the knobs of his machine at the head of the table and seemed unaware of Tony's predicament.

'How old is the little boy?' she asked.

'Just turned two. He's had a suspicion of a hernia since birth, but we didn't expect it to flare up quite so dramatically.'

The child had appeared to be asleep, under the influence of his pre-operative medication, but at the sound of their voices he opened his eyes and looked straight up at Tony. He gave a small smile, as though satisfied with what he saw, then closed his eyes again. Sam heard Tony draw a short, sharp breath and she turned and looked straight at him, willing him to snap out of his freeze before everyone else in the theatre became aware of it too.

He was still very pale, but he moved closer to the table and raised a hand to place it on the child's abdomen. As his fingers touched the firm, smooth flesh, he hesitated, then began a gentle probing. After a minute, he said, 'Right! Go ahead, Charles. We'll scrub.'

Charles, busy preparing the injection he would give to begin the anaesthesia, merely nodded. Sam followed Tony through into the scrub-room. He seemed completely unaware of her presence as they turned on taps, soaped their arms and hands and began to wield their brushes rhythmically. After a while, in another attempt to help him back to normality, she said quietly, 'It'll be all right, you know.'

He looked round at her and she was appalled to see the misery in his eyes as he said, 'Sister Hayes, you have no idea what you're talking about. It will never be all right—never, ever!'

Sam had a feeling it would not help matters to press things further just now, so she concentrated, silently, on her scrubbing, feeling puzzled and concerned for him. The immediate thing was to get him through the operation, and she still felt far from confident that he could manage that.

But when, gowned and gloved, they moved to the operating table, he seemed to have himself under control, although Sam sensed a tenseness in him as he painted the child's abdomen with antiseptic lotion and helped Sam position the sterile drapes.

Sam was feeling tense and edgy too, but now it was for him and not for herself. In fact, she had completely ceased to think about her own ability to cope. A child's life was in Tony's hands. If he froze completely she had no idea whether Charles Welsh was competent to take over. Charles had sutured her leg, of course, so he must have some degree of surgical know-how. She found herself praying, silently, urgently, that Tony would not make a botch of things.

She handed him a scalpel and waited tensely to see what would happen. It was only after he had made the initial incision with a steady hand that she realised she had been holding her breath. But the worst was over now. That first incision, of the skin, was always the worst moment in OR for anyone who was feeling less than confident. If you survived that, you would almost certainly survive what followed. Tony was going to be all right.

Even when, a few minutes later, he threw a pair of artery forceps to the floor, saying they were antiquated and should have been replaced long ago, she wasn't unduly worried, recognising that he was simply releasing a safety valve and would feel all the better for having done so. Certainly she didn't allow it to disturb her concentration.

And she was finding she *had* to concentrate. Although the procedure was simple and relatively short, two factors had her on her toes—she was working with a surgeon whose habits and preferences were unfamiliar to her, and it really was too long since she had done OR work.

If Tony had been behaving normally, he could have helped her by telling her what he required as they went along. Most of it was fairly standard, of course—scalpels, retractors, clamps, sponges... She hesitated between the straight and curved Mayo scissors that Sister Benson had put on the trolley, then handed him the curved ones. He frowned, and Sam hoped they too were not going to end up on the floor. But, with a visible attempt at restraint, he said quietly, 'I prefer straight Mayos, as a rule.'

'Sorry!' Sam said, and, encouraged by his apparent return to normality, asked, 'What catgut do you like for the floor of the inguinal canal, Doctor?'

'Two O chromic, please, Sister.'

With the crisis seemingly over, the sense of relief in Theatre was almost tangible. Sam thought Tony must surely be aware of it. Perhaps he was, because from then on he seemed quite relaxed, discussing with Charles Welsh another patient in whom they had a mutual interest, and then various aspects of the hospital barbecue.

The only thing that seemed to Sam to be not quite normal was the alacrity with which he turned away from the table when the last suture was in place, saying crisply, 'Fix the dressing, please, Sister.' Without further ado he left the theatre.

It took Sam only a matter of seconds to cover the wound with a dressing and tape it in place. Then she

murmured, 'Excuse me, I must see to. . .' and hurried
out, removing gloves and mask as she went. Those left
behind in Theatre would be occupied for some time
transferring the patient to Recovery. Time enough for
her to catch up with Tony.

She had no idea what she would say to him when she
did so, but she quite desperately wanted to be there, in
the unlikely event that he wanted to talk about what had
happened to him during surgery.

His theatre garb lay in an untidy heap on the scrub-
room floor. She found him sitting with his head in his
hands in the duty-room. He didn't look up as she
hesitated just inside the door, until she asked, 'Can I
help in any way?'

He turned then and looked at her, but seemed to be
having difficulty remembering who she was. At length
he shook his head and got heavily to his feet. She
thought he was going to leave without saying anything,
but, just before he reached the door, he turned and said,
'I'm almost tempted to take you up on your offer. But
this is my problem, and I'd hate myself even more than
I do now if I laid it on you.'

'My shoulders are broad,' she assured him. He looked
at her with a sceptical grunt and she added quickly,
'Figuratively, anyway.'

'Again, thanks, but no.' He flicked a wrist and looked
at his watch. 'While I'm here I might as well do a round.
And you? How come you're in Theatre?'

'Matron called me on. She's short-staffed because of
the flu.'

He said quickly, 'Don't you go catching it,' and
sounded as though he really cared.

'I'm pretty tough.'

He laughed and said, '"Broad-shouldered",
"tough"—some day I'll have to talk to you about your
self-image!' He stretched out his hand and just touched

her on the shoulder, with a fleeting smile, before walking out of the duty-room.

Sam exhaled a long breath and, feeling somewhat relieved, went back to the theatre to help with the cleaning up and see that the girls took their proper breakfast break.

As she approached, she could hear them talking, their voices raised above the noise of running water and the clattering of bowls.

'It was quite dicey in there for a while, wasn't it?' Maisie Jenkins was saying.

'Really was! I'm surprised he's let it get to him so much. After all, his wife's hardly been round the place for months.'

So his divorce was common knowledge, thought Sam. She dropped a couple of artery forceps into a tray to announce her presence and the voices next door stopped immediately.

Sam was inclined to agree with the girls. Tony Larsen had had plenty of time to get used to the idea that his marriage was on the rocks. He'd told her himself, the night of the barbecue, that it was only a matter of time. She had felt then that he was having difficulty handling the thought of divorce because he was still in love with his wife, and his behaviour this morning had served to confirm that conviction.

She carried her tray of instruments through into the ante-room. The two nurses looked at her curiously. She had met them both when she was a patient, but this was the first time she had worked with either of them. They were still not quite at ease with her and she guessed they were wondering whether it was wise to say anything to her about Dr Larsen's behaviour this morning. Sam, on her part, was curious to know whether that behaviour was atypical, or whether he was subject to fits of temperament in Theatre.

The nurses came and went, doing the routine cleaning up. They exchanged a few platitudes with Sam and then Sandi Jones, a little bright-eyed, red-haired aide, spoke up.

'Do you think Dr Larsen wasn't feeling well this morning, Sister?'

'I've really no idea. He certainly did seem a bit tense once or twice.'

'That's putting it mildly! I thought he was really on the edge.'

'He isn't always like that, then?' queried Sam.

'He can be a bit moody at times, but usually he's a lamb.' Emboldened, Sandi added, 'I guess it's understandable—what with the divorce and everything.'

Sam wondered whether Sandi's 'everything' meant something or nothing, but she shouldn't be encouraging the nurses to gossip, so she just said, 'Perhaps so,' a little repressively and concentrated on removing a scalpel blade from its handle. The girls took the hint and nothing more was said.

Sam went to breakfast feeling utterly exhausted. As she helped herself to cornflakes in a virtually empty dining-room, a nurse dropped in with a message from Matron that Sister Hayes was to go off duty for the rest of the day. Sam had to admit she was grateful. Normally she could spend all day on duty and half the night dancing without feeling as whacked as she did now.

Thunder was rolling overhead as she crossed the lawn back to the home, and as she dropped on to her bed she could hear rain pelting down and thought how glad the farmers would be. It was two o'clock before she woke— again in response to a knock on her door and the information that she was wanted on the phone.

She slipped into her robe and staggered along, bare-footed and only half awake, to the nurses' sitting-room. When she heard Tony's voice, her first thought was that he had rung up to find out why she was not at work on his project. She was wrong.

He was seeing patients in his rooms, he said, would be finished about three o'clock and was wondering whether he could pick her up from the hospital shortly thereafter and take her out to renew acquaintance with Bridie. After that, if she agreed, he would very much like to take her to dinner, somewhere in town.

He didn't make any reference to the events of that morning and his voice sounded perfectly normal, but Sam was sure his invitation was in the nature of an olive branch. She almost accepted without ado, but a small inner voice urged caution. Would it be wise to be seen dining in public with a man who was in the throes of a divorce? She suspected that her scruples arose largely from the fact that she believed he was still in love with his wife.

Misinterpreting her hesitation, he said, with a rueful laugh, 'I promise I won't throw the cutlery across the room.'

'It's not that,' she assured him. 'It's just that. . .well, I don't know much about the mores of a small Australian town. What would people think. . .?'

'You mean because I'm a married man, even if only pro tem?'

'Exactly.'

'I can assure you nobody would think twice about it. People here are used to my wife being anywhere but here, and they treat me like a single—find partners for me for parties and things. No one raises an eyebrow if they see me squiring a pretty lady about town occasionally.'

She wondered how often was 'occasionally', and whether any of the 'pretty ladies' would have reasons of their own for resenting her being squired about town by him. Not that *that* worried her unduly.

'In that case, thank you, I'd love to come.' Then, in case she had sounded too enthusiastic, she added quickly, 'I've been hoping to see Bridie again before I leave.'

He took her up on that at once. 'Before you leave? Have you changed your plans to stay?'

'Oh, no!' she assured him, pleased at the concern she heard in his voice. Then she realised the cause of that concern, and added, 'I'm enjoying working on your project. I really hope to get a lot more of it done, now that I've begun to master the word processor.'

'Yes, well, we can talk about that later. May I pick you up at three-fifteen?'

'I'll be ready.'

Three-fifteen! Just an hour! Even with an adequate wardrobe, she'd have had a problem finding something versatile enough to cover a visit to a farm to see a horse, and dinner with a doctor somewhere in town, probably at a hotel. If she had more time, she could rush downtown and see what the shops had to offer. She surveyed the contents of her wardrobe with dismay. Her ethnic-looking blouse would do, if she had something to dress it up with. What it needed was silk trousers, preferably wide-leg, and black. She didn't possess any. But Louise did!

She raced back to the sitting-room and rang through to the hospital, only to be told that Louise was in Maternity and unavailable. Thinking that desperate situations demanded desperate measures, Sam scooted along to Louise's room, and knowing exactly how it felt to be a thief, extracted Louise's black silk pants from the wardrobe, appeasing her conscience somewhat by scrawling a note on an envelope on Louise's table:

Had a sudden urgent need for some glam gear. Have borrowed your black pants—hope you don't mind. Sam.

Then she just had time for a quick shower and a careful make-up.

Tony's look of approval when she met him at the door assured her that her frantic efforts had been worthwhile. His car was a pale grey Volvo. He held the door as she slid into the passenger-seat and, as he walked around to get behind the wheel, she thought he looked most presentable himself, in dark blue trousers and a crisp white shirt with blue stripes.

He turned and smiled at her before he switched on the ignition. And there it was again—that 'God's-in-his-heaven, All's-right-with-the-world' feeling she so often had in his presence.

They talked happily about nothing very much on the way out to East Winds. Tony explained that his present domestic arrangements precluded him from asking her to eat at his place.

'Not that I'm not a dab hand at producing a passable meal,' he told her with a smile. 'Time is the real problem—never enough of it. You don't know what a lift it gives me to think that my project is going ahead at last. I'd just about consigned it to the "some time, never" basket.

'If I continue to get calls to the hospital it may have to stay there,' Sam reminded him, hoping he might take that as a cue to talk about that morning in OR. He was silent for a time, but when he spoke again it was about Bridie, and then they were laughing together about Sam having mistakenly supposed that Bridie was his wife.

In the big, cool sitting-room of the homestead, Tony poured drinks and, as they sat sipping, he asked her about her home in England and her parents. They compared notes on the ski-fields they had been to in Europe and he told her he was looking forward to attending a medical conference in Bangkok in a couple of weeks' time. Sam said she had missed seeing Bangkok

on her way out, but hoped to see it on her return flight.
Tony said he knew it quite well, as he had close friends
living and working there.

Their drinks finished, he held out a hand to help her
to her feet, and as they walked through the house and
across the grass to see Bridie, it seemed perfectly natural
for him to keep her hand in his. And not only natural,
but nice.

The earlier storm had cleared the air, and, although it
still wasn't cool by English standards, it was fresh and
pleasant. Tony led her right into the paddock this time
and told her the names of each of the three horses who
came across to them. He greeted each of them with a pat
and a friendly word, but it was clear that Bridie held
first place in his affections. Sam could see why. It wasn't
only that Bridie was a splendid-looking animal, but she
had such intelligent eyes and a friendly, almost playful
disposition. Sam quite fell in love with her.

As they stood with the horses, Tony told Sam more
about his property. By local standards, it was little more
than a hobby farm, but even so, he had to leave most of
the running of it to a neighbour on a share-farm basis,
because of his commitment to his profession. He talked
freely about both his farming and medical interests, and
even mentioned Trish's name a couple of times, without
apparent bitterness. But he said nothing at all about his
life before coming to Wirrando two years ago.

Back at the house, he told Sam he had made early
reservations for dinner at the local hotel because he
realised she had been up early that morning and he was
still concerned about her ability to cope with a long day.

Sam went to the bathroom to freshen up before
leaving, and when she returned to the sitting-room, her
footsteps noiseless on the thick-pile carpet, Tony was
standing gazing at what was clearly a photograph in his
hand. In fact, he was so absorbed in it that she was able

to stand for several seconds, watching him. The brooding look was on his face again, and Sam knew intuitively that the photograph in his hand was of his wife, and the look of suffering on his face could mean only one thing.

Not wishing him to know she had seen him at such a moment, she retreated a few steps and snapped the catch of her handbag as she approached the door again. She began to talk immediately, saying something to the effect that there seemed to be only the one hotel in town, and saw him slip the photograph back into his wallet, which, in turn, was returned to his pocket.

So he carried the photograph with him. Suddenly the brightness faded from her day and she had to make a determined effort to keep up her side of the conversation on the way back into town, in case he noticed that something was amiss. Not that that was difficult—he was much more subdued himself and made only one or two half-hearted attempts to introduce subjects of interest to her.

It seemed farmers generally ate early, because there were already several parties seated at tables in the big dining-room of the hotel. Most of the diners greeted Tony as he passed, and several spoke to Sam too, remembering her from the barbecue night. Tony introduced her to others.

It wasn't until they were well into their meal that he mentioned that morning in Theatre.

'I want to apologise,' he said, 'and to thank you.'

She tried to wave that aside, but he persisted. 'It was your steadiness that got me through, and I'm grateful,' he said, and reached a hand across the table to cover hers.

Sam knew she shouldn't place too much significance on these small gestures he made with such ease. She was, after all, only one of many ladies he squired about town in this interim period while he waited for the reconciliation with his wife that he hoped would come. She herself was still here in Wirrando only because he needed a typist to work on his research project.

But she liked the feel of her hand in his, so she allowed it to remain where it was until the waiter came to clear their main course.

When the waiter had gone, Tony began to talk about his past. Sam sensed that he was leading up to something, and that it had some connection with what had happened that morning in Theatre. This time he went back beyond the two years he had been in Wirrando.

'My father was a doctor,' he said. 'A cardiologist—and a good one. He could detect a predisposition to cardiac disease long before anyone else could. In his patients, that is—not in himself. His colleagues, and his family, tried to warn him about what his stressful life was doing to him, but he wouldn't listen—didn't have time to sit still long enough to do so. He died of a massive infarction while I was still in medical school.'

'I'm sorry.'

He looked at her, nodded and went on with his story. 'At first, his death inspired me to greater effort. I was determined to fill his shoes, and it was years before I recognised that I was on the same treadmill as he had been, and unless I got off it I'd end up with my name on a gravestone beside his.'

He was silent, remembering.

'And. . .?' Sam prompted.

'We moved to the country. In New South Wales—not exactly Back o' Bourke, but a totally different lifestyle. I was surprised to discover how much country life appealed to me.'

Again, a long silence. Sam thought, if only she could fill in the gaps—know what was going through his mind right now, she would have the key to the man, would

know why he was what he so often was—brooding,
morose, haunted. . .

'So what made you come to Wirrando eventually?' she
asked.

He looked at her for a long time. She could sense some
battle being waged within himself. When he did begin
to talk again, it was smoothly, easily, and she knew that
what she was hearing was only the unimportant details
of his life story. She knew he had been right at the point
of telling her the whole of it, and then she would have
understood him and why he was what he was. But
apparently he didn't trust her enough for that.

She listened, without a great deal of interest, to his
account of life in Wirrando, of establishing his farm, of
the problems of being both a doctor and a farmer.

There was no more magic that evening. In fact, Sam
felt quite relieved when it came to an end with Tony
dropping her at the door of the nurses' home. It was just
nine o'clock. His 'Thank you,' was perfunctory and she
knew he was as glad as she was to say goodnight.

She went inside and, rather than sit and ponder the
imponderable about Tony, went in search of Louise, to
thank her for the loan of her trousers and tell her about
her date. There was really no need to omit anything, she
thought despondently. Except, perhaps, the bit about
the photograph. Eventually she told Louise about that
too, and Louise agreed that it was evident Tony still
loved his wife, 'Though, goodness knows, the woman
doesn't deserve it—doesn't know when she's well off.'

Tony went home, calling himself all sorts of names,
from a wimp to a coward, for having stalled at his jump.
He had fully intended telling Samantha everything, but,
when the time came, had found he simply couldn't do it.

Somewhere about two a.m., he decided he was glad
he hadn't. After all, she was only a passing acquaintance—here today, gone tomorrow. Why should he tell

her things about himself that nobody else in Wirrando knew? He'd come here to forget the past. Yes, he was glad he hadn't confided in Samantha Hayes—couldn't understand why he had been tempted to. It was her eyes, he told himself, and the way she looked at a guy. One couldn't help but feel she'd understand—the way she had seemed to understand, yesterday morning, in Theatre. . .

For the next two weeks, Sam was rostered for duty at the hospital, as one nurse after another went down with the flu. The hospital's beds were full, mainly with very old or very young patients with complications of flu. Tony seemed to be continually at the hospital and Sam saw him several times a day, but they were both too busy to talk about anything but hospital matters.

Then one morning Sam woke up with a splitting headache and knew she had succumbed to the virus too. Matron and Tony came to see her and they both seemed to be blaming themselves for having allowed her to work so hard too soon after her accident. Tony said, and Matron fully agreed, that she should take two weeks' sick leave. Sam insisted that she could at least do some work on his project once she was over the worst—she had been feeling guilty that she had done nothing in that regard for so long. But Tony and Matron were adamant—complete R and R for two weeks—longer if they were not completely satisfied about her at that stage.

Sam felt too ill to do anything but obey Tony's orders for the first few days. Then, as she began to feel better, she quite enjoyed having time to read and watch television and chat with the nurses who popped in whenever they were off duty. By the end of the week she was frantic with boredom and told Tony she simply couldn't live like this for another week. He was sympathetic, but unyielding.

That afternoon he came again, and without a nurse, which meant it was a social call. Her door was ajar and he caught her doing aerobics to a children's programme on television. She laughed up at him as she bent to switch off the set. '*Now* do you believe that I'm bored out of my brain?' she asked.

'I believed you this morning. That's why I'm here now, actually.'

She brightened. 'I can go back to work?'

'Better even than that.'

'The way I feel at present, nothing could be better than that!'

'Don't be too sure. How would you rate a trip to Bangkok?'

Her eyes widened. 'I beg your pardon?'

'As I think I told you, I have to go to a medical conference in Bangkok for four days. I'm suggesting that you come too. The climate in Thailand has an excellent reputation for speeding up convalescences, and Bangkok is a sure cure for boredom.' Tony spoke as matter-of-factly as if he were prescribing aspirin for a headache. But his eyes were on her face and she knew he was watching her reaction closely. She mustn't let him see just how excited she was by his suggestion.

'You'd want me to go as your secretary—take notes, that sort of thing?' she asked.

He shrugged. 'You can take notes if you want to. But people tend to assume that secretaries at international conferences are—er——'

'And there would be no—er——' It was as much a statement as a question.

'Definitely no—er——'

With that aspect of the invitation apparently settled to their mutual satisfaction, Sam said, 'If I weren't going in an official capacity I would pay my own way.'

'Absolutely not!'

'Then thank you, but no, thank you.'

'You're one stubborn lady.'

She nodded agreement and he shrugged helplessly. 'Can you afford it? It would only be the fare. I'll be staying with friends in Bangkok and I'm sure they'll be delighted to have you too.'

'Much as he pretended not to approve of it, Daddy has underwritten my "traipsing around" most generously,' Sam assured him.

'Then you'll come?'

'I didn't say that. I need time to think about it.'

'I'm afraid there isn't much time. I leave the day after tomorrow. I'd have to get you on the flights I'm booked on or rearrange them. And I'd need to fax Steve and Lena to let them know you're coming too.' He frowned. 'I really should have thought of it earlier.'

Sam was glad he hadn't. If she had had more time, she would have had to listen to the voice of reason telling her just why she shouldn't even contemplate spending four days in a place like Bangkok with a man she was becoming far too infatuated with. She made just one small concession to sanity.

'Bangkok,' she said. 'That's almost halfway home. Perhaps I should go on from there. . .' Now *she* was watching for *his* reaction.

'As you wish, of course,' he said carefully. But she knew, with a small *frisson* of delight, that he wasn't pleased with the suggestion.

She appeared to reconsider. 'It would mean, of course, that I couldn't do any more work on your project.'

'That would be disappointing, but, as I said, it's up to you.'

'And I did tell Matron I would stay for three months, or until she can get more staff.'

He nodded solemn agreement.

'So, when do we leave?' she asked, and saw his face brighten.

'I'll let you know as soon as I've arranged flights. I know you won't regret having decided to go. Bangkok is a fascinating place.'

He smiled at her and she smiled back.

She didn't tell him that so far she had not spared a thought for the attractions of Bangkok.

CHAPTER EIGHT

TONY must have gone straight to a phone when he left her room, because five minutes later he rang to say that everything was arranged for the day after tomorrow.

That must mean, Sam thought, that he was as elated as she was by the prospect of them spending four days together in Bangkok. Then she told herself sternly that it more likely meant that he was due in surgery any minute and had made the call now in case it slipped his mind later. In any case, the major barrier to a developing. . .friendship between them—she wouldn't let herself entertain the word 'relationship' for more than a fleeting second—remained.

The man was married.

Friendship was, and must remain, the name of the game between them. She must be thankful for that much and not hope for more. No daydreams, no fantasising. But that didn't mean she couldn't feel ridiculously happy and excited as she planned what she would take with her and packed her case.

They flew by the Air Commuter service across the Gulf to Adelaide in under an hour, and just had time to transfer to the international terminal and complete departure formalities before their call came to board the Qantas 747 for Singapore and Bangkok.

Tony had been so quiet all morning that, as Sam sat in her window seat, gazing out at the receding hills, she had a sinking feeling that maybe she should not have accepted his invitation after all. Then she felt his hand on hers and turned towards him with a smile of relief.

'You're thinking I'm not much of a travelling companion,' he observed.

'I was beginning to wonder whether you were having second thoughts about asking me,' she admitted.

The shake of his head and the look in his eyes were eloquent and convincing. 'It's just that I've been trying to get my thoughts together for the paper I'll be giving at the conference. Thanks to the flu epidemic I haven't had much time for preparation, and I doubt that I can "tap-dance" for forty minutes in front of two hundred of the world's leading physicians.'

Sam said warmly, 'I think it's an honour for a doctor from a small country town in outback Australia to be asked to address. . .' Her voice trailed away as she realised that what she had said sounded slightly derogatory. She attempted to backtrack. 'Not meaning, of course, that you're. . .'

Tony laughed. 'A small-time GP from a hick country town.'

Sam blushed. 'One can't deny the "hick country town" bit, but you're only a small-time GP because that's the way you want it.'

He nodded. 'And I never expected to enjoy it as much as I have. There are all kinds of unexpected bonuses too—like attractive strays dropping in unexpectedly.'

They exchanged a smile, then Sam asked, 'How long have you spent in Thailand previously?'

'Twelve months. When I was young and full of high ideals, I spent time in the Volunteer Medical Corps in Cambodian refugee camps, just inside the Thai border.'

Sam was stunned. Tony Larsen was even less of a hick country GP than she had suspected.

Tony sensed her amazement and shrugged in self-disparagement. 'As I said, it was at a stage in my medical career when I still had a burning vision of healing the world. Steve and I did a stint in Thailand together. That's when we became such firm friends, and when I developed the technique for treating one or two of the common skin infections you get in the camps that I'll be speaking about at the conference. It's a technique that's still used in a few places around the world.'

Here was another surprise. 'So you're not speaking on your cardiology research at all?'

He shook his head, then turned to speak to a flight attendant who was offering drinks, before raising his eyebrows questioningly at Sam.

'A gin and tonic, please,' she said.

'And a light ale for me,' said Tony.

As Sam accepted her glass she asked the attendant, 'What time do we arrive in Bangkok?'

'About nine-thirty, local time. After the shops have shut, unfortunately. You're English, aren't you? Are you stopping over in Bangkok or going on to London?'

Sam, still with more than half her mind on what she had just learned about Tony, replied, 'London. . .sorry. . .make that Bangkok.'

Tony looked at her and smiled ruefully. 'I suspect that, given half a chance, she'd go right on. An English rose with her heart in the homeland! A poor colonial doesn't stand a chance!'

The flight attendant looked at Tony, smiled and said, 'I don't think *I'd* have too many problems choosing. Ah, well! Enjoy your stay in Bangkok.'

She departed, and Tony immediately bent down and picked up his briefcase from under the seat. He extracted a clipboard from it, took a pen from his pocket and began scribbling, as though capturing thoughts that were in the back of his mind. Sam's mind was entertaining thoughts of its own about English roses and Australian colonials and glamorous flight attendants.

Tony remained absorbed in his writing until the dinner trolley arrived. They both chose a seafood cocktail. Tony selected a fillet of beef teriyaki to follow, saying he had a weakness for ginger sauce, and Sam opted for chicken with avocado and macadamias. As they ate they talked, comfortably, easily.

Sam found herself thinking that already, on this flight, she had learned quite a lot more about Tony Larsen. He was neither the short-tempered, ill-mannered man she had first encountered at the hospital, nor the tormented surgeon throwing instruments on the floor. Nor, yet again, the bitterly passionate man who had kissed her in the library of his home. Or was he a little bit of all of those? Somewhere, there had to be a clue to the widely differing facets of his personality.

He caught her eye, smiled and said, 'A penny for them?'

She replied lightly, 'I was having obscure thoughts about Dr Jekyll and Mr Hyde.'

'Oh?' His eyes challenged her to explain.

Greatly daring, she elucidated, 'I wonder whether, in your case, it shouldn't be Mr Jekyll and Dr Hyde.'

The smile was still there, but slightly fixed now. 'Go on.'

She floundered a little but continued, 'It's just that I seem to have found you so much more pleasant as a man than as a doctor. . .'

'I didn't realise there was such a difference.'

She thought rapidly. Aware that she hadn't been completely blameless herself in their first encounter, she decided to avoid mentioning that. She didn't want to refer to the incident in the theatre the day he had frozen up. So she side-stepped marginally and said, sketching quote marks in the air, '"Is this how you always react to setbacks?"'

He looked puzzled for a moment, before comprehension and dismay dawned simultaneously in his face.

'You surely didn't think. . .when I said that. . .? Oh, oh! I can see you did!' He turned towards her purposefully. 'I think I can reclaim my reputation on *that* point. All I intended when I asked you that after your accident was to find out whether you were normally a person who resorted to tears at the drop of a hat, or whether they were a symptom of your condition at the time. In other words, I was being clinical, but you took it personally. I'm sorry—I should have realised. . .'

'I admit I was abnormally sensitive at the time, but I did think there was something lacking in your attitude towards me, as a patient.'

He looked at her for a long moment. 'I had my reasons for that, but I shouldn't have let them affect my professional behaviour. And please, don't ask me to tell you what those reasons were.'

She knew by the firmness in his voice that it would be useless to do so, so she merely said, 'I'm sorry I reacted so strongly at the time.'

Tony shook his head in instant denial. 'I should be the one apologising for being an insensitive boor.' He scooped up a rose cut from a tomato, deftly placed it on the end of a toothpick and presented it to her as though it were a dozen of the finest red roses. 'Can you find it in your heart to forgive me, ma'am?'

She laughed. 'Kind sir, I'm quite overwhelmed,' she said, but kept her eyes lowered in case he saw how much his absurd offering had affected her.

She had got precisely nowhere in her attempt to solve the enigma that was Dr Tony Larsen, but she knew that if she persisted he would retire still further into his shell.

As it was, he was very quiet for the remainder of their meal. Had Sam but known it, he was reaffirming a promise he had made to himself, to allow nothing—not the past, not his impending divorce or the prospect of a bleak future—to spoil these precious four days Samantha had, amazingly, agreed to spend with him.

* * *

The heat that greeted Sam and Tony as they stepped from the recently built arrivals hall in Bangkok at the end of their ten-hour flight almost stopped them in their tracks.

'Phew!' breathed Tony. 'I'd forgotten just how hot it can be, even at this time of night. Now where, I wonder, is Steve?'

On the plane, Tony had told Sam about Steve, his long-time friend, and Lena, Steve's wife, a Swedish chemist he had met in Thailand, who was expecting their first child very soon.

Sam frowned. 'I hope we haven't come at a bad time for Lena. If I'd known she was so late in pregnancy, I'd have thought twice about coming. She could even have gone into labour!'

'More likely Steve's stuck in a traffic jam. They can be horrendous in Bangkok. If you're OK for a minute, I'll slip inside and change some money and see if I can find a phone.'

She nodded, feeling suddenly weary, and he reached a hand and touched her gently on the cheek. 'Don't worry, I'm sure everything's fine.'

He moved off quickly, leaving Sam to explain to yet another taxi-driver that no, she didn't want a taxi.

Only a few minutes passed before Tony emerged from the crowd again. He was carrying a bottle of soda water, which he handed to Sam, and was accompanied by a very tall, obviously Australian man, with dark brown hair and a profusion of freckles.

Tony slipped an arm round Sam's waist as he introduced her to Steve. Sam felt a little uncomfortable under the keen eye of the tall Australian, and hoped he wasn't assuming too much about her relationship with Tony. She held out her hand and Steve shook it heartily.

'She's even more gorgeous than you let on, mate,' he said.

Sam looked up at Tony, half in surprise and half in embarrassed reproach. He returned her look blandly.

'Sorry I'm late,' continued Steve. 'However much time you allow to get to the airport in Bangkok, you'll always be late. We'd better get a move on. There's a rather large lady at home who's dying to meet you, Sam, not to mention to see this cad again.' He thumped Tony on the arm, then turned and led them down the stairs to the car park.

A few minutes later Sam was ensconced in the plush leather seat in the back of Steve's BMW, sipping her cold drink and luxuriating in the car's air-conditioning. She had insisted that Tony sit in front with Steve so they could do the catching up they were obviously eager to do. After a while, she took advantage of a break in the conversation to ask, 'Do you live far from the centre of Bangkok, Steve?'

Steve looked back over his shoulder momentarily. 'It's actually rather difficult to say just where the CBD is. We live about fifteen minutes' drive from my office, which is on top of the SOGO shopping centre.'

'The traffic seems even worse since I was here last,' Tony observed.

Sam watched the curious mix of Eastern and Western cultures flashing by as they sped along the freeway. One minute they would be passing a block of new condominiums or a billboard advertising French perfume, and the next moment the freeway would be flying over dimly lit slum areas.

A few minutes passed while Steve and Tony swapped old medical stories. As they left the freeway and battled through the traffic, Steve called out to Sam, 'We're turning into Nang Linchi Road—worth remembering if you're trying to find our place in a cab. Our *soi* is just up ahead.'

Steve spun the car into a side-street and slowed as

they approached a large set of iron gates. A uniformed guard stepped forward and swung the gates open. They drove for another minute or two, past two luxurious apartment blocks and two or three houses hidden behind high walls.

'That's us just up ahead,' Steve remarked, before turning slowly through another set of gates. He stopped the car at the entrance to an eight- or nine-storey apartment block. A guard seated behind a counter barely looked up from the magazine he was reading.

Steve helped unload the bags and then drove the car to a park behind the building.

'I don't know about you, but I'm starting to feel a little jaded,' remarked Tony while they were waiting for Steve to reappear.

Sam nodded. 'It *has* been a long day. I guess it's after midnight back in South Australia.'

Tony slipped an arm around her and his hand tightened on her shoulder. Although gestures such as this were becoming increasingly frequent, Sam knew better than to think they betokened anything more than a growing friendliness between them.

'I'm afraid it will be a while yet before you can get to bed—Steve said Lena and their housekeeper have supper prepared for us,' Tony said. 'But we can sleep in as long as we like in the morning.'

Hazy with fatigue as she was, Sam thought that last statement of his had a nice ring about it. But before she could analyse it, Steve emerged from the lift and said, 'Follow on, you two. Lena will be waiting.'

Steve and Lena's apartment was one of two on the fourth floor. Steve ushered them into a large reception area, cool and inviting, with dark polished wood floors. Through an open door Sam glimpsed an enormous living-room, decorated in white with muted pastel tonings.

Tony whistled. 'Looks like I'm in the wrong game!'

'Tony!'

'Lena!'

Tony turned to embrace a very attractive, very blonde, very pregnant woman who had emerged through a door on their left. She returned his embrace warmly, then looked at Sam. 'You must be Samantha. Welcome to Bangkok. You must be tired. Come and sit down.'

'Thank you. I am, rather.'

Lena led her into the living-room, leaving the men discussing the relative merits of a cold beer or a glass of wine. Tony produced from his bag two bottles of Penfold's St Henri claret, which he knew was an old favourite of Steve's. The men decided to leave the wine for a more auspicious occasion, and settled on a beer.

No sooner had Sam sunk into one of the soft, inviting sofas than the housekeeper emerged, bearing a tray on which were a steaming pot of tea and a dish of small pastries.

'If you're like me,' began Lena, 'all I feel like after a long flight is a cup of tea, and I seem to be particularly addicted now that Junior's so close.' She gave her large stomach an affectionate pat.

'You must be getting excited,' smiled Sam. 'When is the baby due?'

'Another three weeks, although I think at the moment I'm more tired than excited. Steve is the one who's jumping out of his skin—loves to talk about the "fat wife" at home.'

Sam laughed. 'He made some such disrespectful comment at the airport.'

Lena laughed, too, goodnaturedly, and began to stand up, with the obvious intention of pouring the tea, but Sam was on her feet first.

'Please, let me.'

'Thank you. Leaning forward is becoming something

of an impossibility.' Lena eased herself back into the couch and asked, 'Are you very involved in this conference?'

'Oh, no, not at all, really. I've recently had flu, and Tony thought Bangkok was a good place for me to recuperate in.'

Lena smiled. 'And for him to spend a few days with you, away from Wirrando, I suspect!' She glanced over her shoulder at the two men, who were deep in discussion on the terrace. 'Tony's certainly looking happier than I've seen him in years,' she added.

'Oh?'

Sam would have loved to continue this line of conversation with Lena, but at that moment the two men entered from the terrace.

'It's all organised,' announced Steve.

'Is it now!' replied Lena, smiling at Sam. 'I knew we shouldn't have left those two alone for so long—I hate to think what they've hatched up!'

'Pregnant women are so difficult,' Steve complained, dropping on to the couch beside Lena. 'All we thought was that, as Tony only really needs to be at this conference for two days, we should all head off to the Yacht Club on Saturday morning. We can drive back on Sunday night. Plenty of time for them to pack before the flight on Monday morning.'

Lena looked uncomfortable as she shifted in her seat. 'I thought it might be something like that. How do you feel about sailing?' she asked Sam.

'Sounds wonderful,' replied Sam. 'Where's the club?'

'About three hours south of Bangkok, near Pattaya.'

'Oh?'

Steve laughed at Sam's look of surprise. 'I see you've heard a few things about Pattaya.'

'Don't worry,' Lena chimed in. 'The Royal Varuna is a very old-world yacht club, set in its own little bay a thousand miles away from the bright lights of Pattaya, for all intents and purposes.'

'Well,' Tony stood up, 'I don't want to be rude, but I'm ready for bed, and I'm sure Sam is too.'

Lena began to struggle to her feet and Steve was at her side in an instant. 'It's a crane she really needs,' he said with a broad grin.

'I'll have my revenge when it comes to changing nappies at three a.m.' Lena retorted, as they moved off towards the bedrooms, Sam and Tony following.

Lena showed Sam to a bedroom, pointed out the en-suite bathroom, said she hoped Sam slept well and not to get up till she felt like it in the morning, then led Tony further along the hall.

As they went, Sam heard Lena say, 'I wasn't sure. . .' and Tony's quick reply,

'No, this is just right.'

Sam was hanging clothes in her closet a few minutes later when Tony reappeared.

'Everything fine?' he asked.

'Yes. Steve and Lena are delightful, aren't they?' Sam said, and hoped he didn't notice the wistful note in her voice.

'Mmm-hmm. Now, you sleep well.' He hesitated, then moved towards her, placing his hands gently on her shoulders and dropping a kiss on her cheek. 'It's going to be a lovely four days. See you in the morning.'

Bua, Steve and Lena's maid, knocked softly on Sam's door at nine o'clock next morning and entered quietly when Sam called, 'Come in.'

'I'm sorry to disturb you,' she said softly, in good English. 'Dr Larsen is on the phone.'

'On the phone? Where is he?'

'I'm sorry, I do not know. He left early this morning.'

Sam had been awake for almost half an hour. In the

absence of any sounds from next door, she had assumed that Tony was still sleeping. She rolled over and picked up the phone beside her bed.

Tony sounded positively chirpy. 'Enjoying our little sleep-in, are we?'

Sam laughed. 'Yes, Sister Benson! Did I ever tell you what I think of people who are cheerful at this hour of the morning?'

'No. You've never had occasion to,' he teased her. 'But do tell me now. You admire them? Love them, perhaps?'

'No!' she said repressively. 'I find them excessively irritating!'

'Then that's something else I know about you. By the weekend. . .'

'Where are you?' she asked.

'At the Hilton, where the conference is to be held. I woke up at the crack of dawn. Steve dropped me off here and I've been preparing some overhead transparencies and honing my speech. Steve suggetsed I organise with you girls to meet him after work at the Oriental for drinks on the terrace. In the meantime, the day is ours, to do as we like with.'

'Sounds wonderful. What did you have planned?'

'Have you had breakfast yet?'

'No. I thought I'd wait till Lena was up and have breakfast with her.'

'A likely excuse!' he mocked. 'Why don't you leave Lena a note, and come down and have breakfast—well, brunch, I guess, with me, at the Hilton? There's quite a lovely coffee-shop, and we can plan our day. Lena can join us later if she's up to it. Get Bua to write the address of the hotel for the cab-driver.'

'All right. That sounds great.'

'Gotta go. . . I've been trying to catch the conference

organiser all morning. . .see you in the coffee-shop at
ten.'

Sam enjoyed the walk down to Nang Linchi Road. She
wondered about catching a *tuk-tuk*, the brightly coloured
and noisy modern version of a rickshaw. But, even at
this time of day, the idea of an air-conditioned cab was
appealing.

She didn't have to wait long. Bartering for the fare
before getting into the cab seemed strange, and Lena
could probably have got the ride for quite a few *baht* less,
but that didn't matter to Sam this morning, elated as
she was at the idea of spending a day in Bangkok with
Tony.

The coffee-shop at the Hilton was full of recently
arrived delegates to the conference, many of whom
seemed to know Tony. In these circles, he seemed to be
something of a celebrity. He and Sam sat next to the
huge glass wall overlooking the garden and planned
their day.

'I'll be tied up with the conference all day tomorrow,
and, with the trip to the Yacht Club, we really only have
today for sightseeing and shopping in Bangkok. I
thought that, as we're close to some of the best market
areas already, maybe we should shop for a few hours,
then head off to see some temples and the Palace this
afternoon.'

'You're the one who knows Bangkok. I'm in your
hands entirely.'

'What a delightful prospect!' He was teasing her
again. But his voice was quite serious as he reached
forward and stroked her cheek lightly. 'Have I told you
how beautiful you're looking this morning? Asia is
obviously agreeing with you already.'

'Thank you,' she said, and then, rather than let him
see how his touch affected her, she added quickly, 'I

should ring Lena soon, and let her know what we're planning.'

'Come downstairs—we can use the phone there. I meant to say that the second part of the plan was to catch a river boat back, to meet Steve and Lena at the Oriental, for cocktails on the terrace at sixish.'

Sam laughed. 'I should sleep in more often! It sounds as though you and Steve have got this all worked out.'

Sam phoned Lena, who was happy to have a quiet day at home out of the heat but suggested that if they wanted to shop for clothes they head down to the markets at Pratunam, and then back to the air-conditioned comfort of the Sogo or Central department stores for lunch and some more civilised shopping.

The markets at Pratunam were basically a tent city covering a number of city blocks. The heat trapped under the thousands of pieces of canvas that made up the roof was so intense that Sam quickly understood why Lena had suggested retreating to an air-conditioned shopping centre.

The markets were crowded with tourists and Thais alike, and Sam soon found out that, with a little parleying, there were some bargains to be had. When Louise and the other nurses back at Wirrando had learned that she was going to Bangkok, they had plied her with lists of requests for various items of clothing, and of course, it was a marvellous opportunity to replenish her own wardrobe.

Tony stood by patiently, occasionally offering an opinion if Sam asked for one, and allowing himself to be laden with an ever-increasing number of parcels and carrier-bags.

When they passed a stall selling some stylish men's shirts, Sam announced that it was time Tony bought something for himself. He grabbed her hand and insisted they keep moving, but Sam merely turned and, with her free hand, began choosing two or three shirts that appealed to her. As she began bartering with the eager stallholder, Tony playfully tugged on her arm, insisting that he was over-supplied with shirts already.

'Your husband very impatient,' said the stallholder, who was a young Thai boy of no more than twelve.

'He's not my husband, but yes, he *is* very impatient,' Sam replied.

Tony, not in the least abashed at having been taken for Sam's husband, laughed and gave in, to the extent of allowing Sam to hold a shirt up against him to measure for size. That done, he pulled some *baht* from his pocket and said, 'How much?'

Sam pushed his money aside, paid the boy herself, and presented the parcel of shirts to Tony. 'These are a present,' she said, and added lightly, 'You can think of me when you wear them.'

Tony smiled. 'Don't think I won't! And thank you.' He moved all his parcels to one hand and took her hand with his free one. 'I don't know about you, but I'm about ready to retreat to Sogo.'

Tony continued to hold her hand as they battled to find their bearings in the maze of stalls. Eventually they found their way out on to Ratchaprarop Road, and began to head back to Sogo. The road was a moving mass of cars, motorbikes and *tuk-tuks*, which seemed to vanish after only a few hundred yards in the dust and pollution.

Lena's other suggestion had been a restaurant on level four of the shopping centre, where they enjoyed a fabulous meal of prawns in a spicy chilli sauce. Even including the cost of the cold Singha beer they drank, the meal cost less than the price of the drinks alone, back in Australia.

They shopped briefly in Sogo, selecting some baby clothes as a gift for Lena and Steve. Tony, who had so far taken the business of shopping in his stride, even when it had included some items of personal feminine wear, seemed uncomfortable looking at the babywear. Sam could only assume that his patience was finally beginning to run out, and she finished her purchase quickly and announced that she was ready to play tourist. Tony's demeanour improved at once, and as they hailed a cab he began to give her a brief summary of the recent history of Thailand. They spent the next three hours at the Grand Palace, exploring the Temple of the Emerald Buddha, before visiting Wat Po, the old temple that housed the giant reclining Buddha.

Tony had intended that they take a boat ride back down the Chao Phraya River to the Oriental, but by five o'clock his early start that morning was beginning to take its toll.

'Why don't we grab a cab?' he said. ' I don't think I could stand the noise of a "long tail boat", as they're called.'

Tony leant in the window of the first cab to stop, arranged the fare in Thai rather than English, and flung open the rear door for Sam. As he collapsed into the seat beside her, Sam stroked the side of his cheek.

'You look exhausted. We might have taken the "shop till you drop" maxim a little too far.'

'Just yesterday catching up with me.' He turned and looked into her eyes. 'I'd forgotten how tiring all this noise and heat can become. I don't know how you manage to keep looking so wonderful.' Sam felt sure he was about to lean over and kiss her, but something held him back. It might just have been that he knew the Thais frowned on displays of affection in public, but Sam felt it was something more. Either way the moment was lost. And they both knew it.

The cab had slowed in a traffic jam and something in the street caught Tony's eye.

'You see there,' he said, indicating a row of old shops. 'This street, the whole area really, is famous for little antique shops. You can buy some fabulous pieces, but unfortunately you need a permit to take antiques out of the country, so it's strictly window-shopping for us tourists.'

Sam surveyed the row of ageing shops, each displaying a fascinating array of objects in its window.

'I've completely lost my sense of direction. Are we far from the Oriental?' she asked as the cab turned into yet another crowded side street.

'No, not far at all. . . I think,' he replied, peering out, obviously trying to get his bearings. 'In fact. . .'

The cab was slowly moving towards a large white building.

'Is this the Oriental?' asked Sam, trying to hide her obvious disappointment.

Tony laughed as he paid the cab-driver and guided her to the entrance of the hotel.

'This really isn't its best side. After we've met up with the others, I'll show you the old part of the hotel. . .it's quite fascinating.'

Steve and Lena hadn't arrived, so they chose a table on the terrace, seemingly right on the river's edge. The sun was beginning to set, and the river, with its procession of rice barges slowly making their way up-country, was a breathtaking sight.

'I can see why you and Steve organised this. . .it's marvellous!'

'It was Steve's idea, actually. . .but I thought you'd like it. Now what sort of exotic cocktail would you like?'

Sam laughed. 'I know you'll think I'm the most boring person alive, but I *really* feel like a gin and tonic.'

Tony smiled and turned to a waiter hovering nearby.

'My companion and I will have gin and tonics. And maybe a plate of mixed satays. . .in case we get peckish.'

Sitting there on the terrace seemed so perfect that Sam longed to remove that last barrier that always seemed to come between them. She wanted to know about Tony's past, his family, his studies, even his marriage. Somewhere in there was the key. . .not just the key to Tony Larsen, but to what she hoped, more and more, would be a future she would share with him.

Perhaps fortunately, Steve and Lena arrived before she had a chance to say anything. They spent another hour or so recounting the day's sightseeing and shopping before heading off for a quick meal at a local restaurant. Lena was definite that they be back at the apartment early enough for Tony to get a good night's sleep before the conference, a prospect that brought groans from Steve, but a nod of quiet thanks from the others.

CHAPTER NINE

TONY rose early for the conference, slipping a small folder under Sam's door before he left the apartment. It contained a delegate's guest badge with Sam's name on it, and a page from the official programme, with Tony's session times highlighted. Sam had wanted to ask if it would be possible to attend his session of the conference, but this was so much better. Tony wanted her there with him. She felt as though another small barrier had been breached.

Sam slipped quietly into the ballroom at the Hilton Hotel just as the chairman was introducing. . . 'A physician whose work in this area needs little introduction, Dr Anthony Larsen from Australia.' Sam watched in awe as Tony guided the assembly through a brief history of his work in the refugee camps. This was totally divorced from his work at Wirrando. His authority from the lectern, the esteem with which he was held by the conference delegates, left her with a mixture of immense pride and confusion. Why was Tony working in a small bush town like Wirrando? His father's experiences were not explanation enough. If there was to be a future for them, at Wirrando, or anywhere for that matter, she had to know the truth.

'And the paper was well received?' Lena asked later, as they battled the traffic heading south on Sukhumvit Road.

'Well received! The man laid them in the aisles,' replied Steve. 'The wit, the dramatic pauses. . .'

'The *dramatic pauses* were mostly because I couldn't

figure out how to use the controls for the slide machines on the lectern,' laughed Tony.

'I might have known I wouldn't get a straight answer out of either of them,' smiled Lena, twisting uncomfortably so she could see Sam in the back seat.

'He was most impressive,' said Sam.

'Why, thank you,' replied Tony, reaching over and holding Sam's hand.

'In fact, there were moments, if it wasn't for the fact that I've seen him at work, that I was almost convinced he knew what he was talking about.'

That remark earned Sam a playful jab in the ribs from Tony, and a suggestion from Steve that they stop for lunch before things got out of hand in the back seat.

They were just outside Cholbury, still an hour or so from the Yacht Club. A parking attendant, resplendent in a uniform that would have done many a high-ranking officer in the military proud, led them into a parking spot with a series of short blasts from his whistle and an intricate display of hand movements.

Lena made do with some fried rice, while the others shared a jungle curry and some prawns coated in a paste made from chilli and pepper sprigs. Although Sam was a little unsure at first, the prawns were fabulous. . .a delicate, spicy flavour.

Perhaps it was the cooling beer with lunch, or the last remnants of the flu, but Sam felt more than just a little weary as they joined the stream of trucks and cars heading towards Pattaya. Outside was a noisy, dusty mix of the old and the new. One minute they would be passing rice paddies with clusters of dark timber buildings, and the next it would be a vast wasteland, cleared for some new country club or industrial estate.

Inside the quiet of the BMW, though, Sam was content to let the scenery pass by, her head resting softly on Tony's shoulder. She stayed that way, at times almost asleep, until they approached the outskirts of Pattaya. The collection of bars and nightclubs looked innocuous enough in the warm afternoon sun, but Sam could see that it would quickly take on another persona once night fell.

Fortunately, the Royal Varuna Yacht Club was just as Lena had described. Hidden away down a track through some dense undergrowth, the Club sat proudly on its own secluded bay, complete with a small sandy beach, overlooking a group of islands a mile or two offshore.

'This is marvellous!' exclaimed Tony, looking through the open clubhouse at the tangle of masts of the smaller boats pulled up on the sand.

'I'm afraid it's not quite the Hilton, but they're fine for the night,' replied Steve, as he signed for their rooms. 'You can always retreat to our place. . .just through the trees there. . .for a hot shower.'

They arranged to meet back in the bar in half an hour, while there was still enough light to rig Steve's new boat, an Enterprise class racing dinghy, and, with half an ounce of luck, squeeze in a short sail.

The rooms were spartan indeed, but quite in keeping with the tropical setting. . .cane furniture and a slow overhead fan to keep the air moving. Sam removed the one or two items of clothing she had brought with her, and decided to change into a bathing-suit. She wrapped a large beach towel around her waist, and, book in hand, headed back down to the clubhouse. Sam was sure Lena wouldn't be doing any sailing, and, for this afternoon at least, Tony and Steve could have the sailing to themselves. Sam was content to sit in the shade and chat with Lena.

The men already had the boat boys pulling Steve's new pride and joy out of the boat racks. Tony waved from the lawn in front of the clubhouse as he saw Sam take a seat in the shade next to Lena.

'Boys and their boats!' Lena chuckled. 'Steve'll love having Tony here for a sail. His crew hasn't been much use lately,' she said, patting her belly.

Sam thought she looked uncomfortable and asked if she could get her a cushion.

'No, I'm just a bit sore from sitting in the car for so long. It's all getting to be a bit of an effort.'

The afternoon passed slowly by. Sam and Lena talked about Bangkok, Lena's family back in Sweden, how she had met Steve, but, to Sam's dismay, little was said about Tony.

The boys retreated from the heat every now and then to enjoy a beer in the shade of the clubhouse. Steve was pleased with the new rigging and was anxious to get the boat into the water as soon as possible. The wind had been slowly picking up, and, though the bay and the clubhouse were protected, the water beyond was starting to show telltale signs of a storm brewing.

'Wouldn't even be fifteen knots yet,' replied Steve, to the others' concern at his announcement that they were ready for a sail.

'You be careful,' said Sam, as Tony pulled on a life vest.

'We'll be fine,' smiled Tony, leaning over and kissing Sam on the head. 'Besides, if this wind picks up any more, Steve and I will probably be back in Australia before you know it!'

'That's what I'm afraid of,' called Lena, as Steve and Tony battled to hold the small boat into the wind to allow them to raise the sails.

'Do you think they'll be all right?' asked Sam, as she watched the boat crash through the first of the whitecaps.

'Those two have wasted more years mucking around in boats than you'd believe. They'll be fine.'

Steve was revelling in the conditions, but Tony wasn't quite so sure. The boat was keeled over, hard on the wind, about a mile offshore, when Steve shouted 'Ready about!' Tony ducked down from his position leaning out over the gunwale, and grabbed the jib sheet, just as Steve called 'Coming about!' and threw the tiller hard across. There was an almighty crack, and Tony's first thought was that the boom had hit Steve as it had swung across. He jammed the jib sheet into a cleat and spun around. It took a second before Tony realised what had happened. The whole rudder section had broken away under the strain, and Steve, still clutching the tiller, was fast disappearing twenty or thirty feet behind the boat.

Tony knew he had to act quickly. He grabbed the main and jib sheets and, using the sails, slowly turned the boat into the wind. As soon as the boat had slowed, he released the sheets, let the wind spill out of the sails, and brought the boat to a halt. He threw the loose end of the main sheet towards Steve, who was battling his way through the chop, his right hand still clutching the tiller.

'I think something's wrong,' said Lena, watching the stationary boat floundering off the bay. 'Quick, get the boat boys to launch one of the rescue boats!' Sam raced down to the beach and tried to explain what had happened.

'Let go of the tiller, you idiot!' Tony shouted as Steve neared the boat.

'Are you kidding? Do you know how long it took to get these fittings sent out from England?' replied Steve, as he clambered back into the boat.

'Are you OK?'

'Apart from jamming my hand as I went over the

side, I think I'm fine. Glad you remembered what to do
for a man overboard.'

Tony was looking down at Steve's hand. 'That doesn't
look too good to me. You sit down up front and try to
keep it elevated, while I see if I can't get this tub back
to the clubhouse. . .actually, if it's not going to dent your
pride too much, I think a tow from the rescue boat might
be in order,' he said, indicating the fast approaching
rubber duckie.

'You've definitely broken two fingers, but it's damage to
the nerves that I'm more worried about,' said Tony,
looking down at Steve's crushed fingers. 'Sam, try and
get me some ice, and I'll see what the club has in the
way of painkillers in its first aid kit. I'm afraid your
hand's going to be a bit painful by the time we get back
to Bangkok.'

'What? Tonight?' exclaimed Steve. 'I'll be fine. Just
strap it up.'

'Sorry, mate. If the nerves have been crushed, the
sooner we can get you to a micro-surgeon, the better.
Pity—looks as if the storm has blown over. It's going to
be a beautiful sunset,' said Tony, smiling at Sam, who
had arrived back carrying a large bucket of ice.

The trip back to Bangkok was a silent affair, each
absorbed in their own thoughts. Steve, his hand heavily
bandaged in a sling and obviously in pain, was the most
talkative of the lot, reliving the afternoon's adventure
and moaning about the damage to his beloved boat.
Lena and Sam were still a little shell-shocked by the
whole incident and sat quietly in the back, as Tony
battled the traffic on the poorly lit highway.

Tony spoke at length with Steve's doctor when they
arrived back in Bangkok, and it was decided to admit
Steve that night. Tony and Sam were both worried that
a night at the hospital would not be good for Lena, so it

was decided that Tony would go with Steve and Sam would stay with Lena.

The night passed slowly, with Tony ringing to say that Steve would be operated on first thing in the morning and that he would be home as soon as things were organised.

As Bua had been given the weekend off, Sam made Lena a light meal and suggested that she go to bed, with the promise that she would wake her as soon as she heard anything.

It was three a.m. when Tony finally arrived back, to find Sam asleep on the couch. He placed a blanket over her, and kissed her gently before wearily retreating to bed. As he left the room, Sam stirred, smiled and snuggled into the blanket.

The next morning was spent waiting for news from the hospital, and when they finally visited Steve in the afternoon he was on a pethidine drip and still groggy from the surgery. There was no point in staying more than a few minutes and, on the way home, Tony reassured Lena, 'It'll take a while to get full sensation back into those fingers, but he'll eventually have full movement, even if his violin playing suffers a little.'

Lena, in the back seat of the car, laughed a little tremulously. 'That'd be the day! I'm sorry we didn't get a chance to relax at the Club,' she continued, 'but Steve always seems to invite trouble. Sometimes I think my life would be easier if I didn't love him so much.'

Tony glanced sideways at Sam and their eyes met. Then his left hand left the wheel and reached out and covered hers for a moment. She knew he was thinking, as she was—lucky Steve. Lucky Lena. Lucky Sam too, she thought, as Tony pressed her hand before returning his own to the steering-wheel, to have had this few days with him in Bangkok. Perhaps the future would be even kinder to her now. She flushed slightly, remembering his kiss the night before and the happy dreams it had engendered.

They had a quiet, somewhat subdued dinner at home that night, then packed and were in bed before ten in preparation for their early departure the next morning.

In the cab on the way to the airport just after dawn, Tony said, 'It feels as though we'd just got here. I don't know about you, but for me, in spite of all the drama, it's been a very special few days.'

Sam nodded silent agreement.

CHAPTER TEN

'DR LARSEN, there's a message for you. Would you please call the hospital as soon as possible?'

Tony grimaced and looked about the tiny terminal for a public phone.

'Use ours,' said the desk clerk, pushing it towards him.

'Thanks.'

Sam wandered off a short distance, thinking how typical it was of a doctor's life to find an emergency awaiting him on return from a few days away.

Looking about her idly, she saw a notice chalked on a blackboard to the effect that there was a flight to Adelaide scheduled for two hours hence. Probably the plane they had come in on, turning around, she thought, and wondered about the life of a flight attendant.

Tony finished his call and walked quickly over to her.

'We'll have to go, I'm afraid. I'll have our luggage picked up later. Charles wants an urgent consultation on a patient who's developed ARDS following viral pneumonia.'

Sam nodded. Acute Respiratory Distress Syndrome was a complicated condition and could lead to respiratory failure without the appropriate intervention.

Tony said little on the short drive to the hospital. When he pulled up outside the nurses' home, Sam made a move to alight quickly, but he leaned across and, with a finger under her chin, turned her face towards him. For the briefest moment his lips brushed hers. It could hardly be called a kiss, but it was enough to set her heart pounding madly and cause a weakness in her knees so that she stumbled slightly as she got out of the car. She hoped, if Tony were watching, that he would put it down to jet fatigue. But he was already doing a U-turn that made the wheels of his car squeal on the driveway, and he didn't look back as he drove towards the hospital.

Sam almost felt she was wafting along the corridor to her room. Jet lag again, no doubt. It felt odd not having a case to unpack, and she had quite decided that the best way to spend the next few hours was lying on her bed.

But there was a note pinned to her pillow. It was in Louise's handwriting and it read:

Michael (??) is in Adelaide until Friday. He was devastated to hear about your accident and demands to know why wasn't he told?! He sends his love (!!!) and says that he *must*—repeat, *absolutely must*—see you. Please phone him urgently. Louise.

PS I said you were recuperating with a friend— didn't mention Bangkok. Further episodes in this soap opera are eagerly awaited.

Sam chuckled at the typically Louise note. Then she sobered. She had quite forgotten recently that Michael— Michael Platt, with whom she had had an on-off, low-key sort of relationship for the last year or so back in England—was bringing his band to Adelaide for the Festival of Arts and had hoped to meet up with her there. Michael had always wanted more from their relationship than she was prepared to give. She saw now, without a shadow of doubt, that, whatever the future might hold for her, there was only one thing to be done about Michael—break off whatever had been between them, once and for all.

She sat on her bed and thought hard for several minutes.

She could call Michael, of course, on the number he

had left, and which Louise had scrawled at the foot of
the note, but he would hardly be sitting around his hotel
room at this hour of the day; he would be somewhere
practising with the band. And she knew very well that
she would never convince him, over the phone, that she
was serious about terminating whatever relationship
they had once had. The only way to do that would be to
see him in person.

There was no real problem about that, she realised.
She still had two days of sick leave left, and for that time
she was accountable to no one.

Her mind was racing now and every vestige of fatigue
had vanished. She could catch that commuter flight back
to Adelaide, see Michael and return to Wirrando in time
to begin work on Wednesday. Her luggage was already
at the airport. . . She must ring and book a flight. . .call
a taxi. . .write a note. . .

In the end she wrote two notes. One was to Louise,
telling her she was going back to Adelaide—no time to
say more now, she would tell all on her return. The
second note became necessary when, on trying to contact
Tony, she was told that he was still busy with Dr Welsh
and had said they were not to be disturbed. She scrawled
a quick line or two to him, saying much the same as she
had to Louise. After a moment's hesitation, she signed it
'Love, Sam,' and suppressed any qualms she might have
had about doing that by telling herself that it meant no
more than had his kiss this morning, which was almost
nothing.

Time was running out. She put the note to Tony in an
envelope, sealed it and left it with the one to Louise,
with a hasty 'Please deliver' scrawled on it.

By then the taxi was at the door. Collapsed in its back
seat on the way to the airport, she realised that her
fatigue, which had been kept at bay by the excitement
and busyness of the last hour or so, was returning in full

force. She made herself stay awake on the short flight to Adelaide, knowing she would feel even worse if she allowed herself to catnap, and promising herself she would sleep the clock round tonight, wherever she might be. If Eleanor was not at home, she would book into a motel near the city. It was not until the plane was losing height before landing that she remembered that the Festival of Arts was in full swing in Adelaide and motel vacancies would be as scarce as hen's teeth.

While waiting for her luggage to appear on the carousel, she found a phone and rang Eleanor. To her relief, Eleanor answered almost at once, and was surprised and delighted at the prospect of seeing Sam and said, yes, of course they had a bed for her.

'Have a cup of coffee in the terminal. It'll take me less than half an hour to pop down from Skye and collect you.'

'Pop down from Skye!' There was a ring of fantasy about that, quite in keeping with this whole exercise, thought Sam.

Eleanor was as good as her word. In just under thirty minutes she raced into the coffee-shop, greeted Sam with a quick hug and hurried her outside to where her car was standing in a five-minute set-down zone, with the baby's carry-cot strapped into the back seat, under the watchful eye of a tolerant airport official.

They drove through suburbs and then through the city, with Sam exclaiming at beautiful tree-lined North Terrace with, cheek by jowl, Parliament House, Government House, the state library, museum, art gallery, university, hospital, the botanic gardens. Then there were more attractive, tree-filled suburbs and a brief ascent into the foothills before they turned into the driveway of Eleanor's home. It was a large, modern home, set in what was obviously a new suburb, built,

Eleanor told Sam, on what had once been extensive vineyards.

Sam exclaimed again, as she alighted from the car, at the wide panoramic view over the city to the Gulf waters.

'Wait until you see the lights at night,' Eleanor said proudly. 'It's like a fairyland.'

Inside, Eleanor insisted on making more coffee, and she and Sam sat and talked until it was time for her to go and collect the other children from school, leaving the sleeping baby in Sam's care.

Just about that time, Louise was sitting in the easy-chair in her room, still in uniform, reading the note from Sam and finding it excessively frustrating.

Why on earth had Sam gone chasing off to Adelaide like that? Obviously, it was to see that Michael person who had phoned and, in Sam's absence, left his rather peremptory messages for her. Sam had never so much as mentioned a Michael to Louise, but he must mean something to her or she wouldn't have taken off like that at the first crook of his little finger.

Louise was disappointed. Though Sam had never actually said anything, Louise had picked up definite vibes—or thought she had—that had led her to hope that Sam and Tony. . .well, there *was* the divorce, but that would soon be a thing of the past. . .and Tony had asked Sam to stay on at the hospital. . .and then taken her with him to Bangkok. . .

And now here was this Michael appearing out of nowhere, and Sam haring off as though she couldn't get to see him quickly enough.

Louise clicked her tongue. Anyone who knew her would have recognised that that meant she was thinking furiously, as she stared at the envelope in her hand, the one with Tony's name on it.

Her mind was so preoccupied with Tony and her

hopes for his future that, when the phone rang, she was not in the least surprised to hear his voice.

He dispensed with the amenities and plunged into what was on his mind. 'Lou, I've been trying to track Samantha down, but all I've been able to get is some fandangled rumour that she went off to catch a plane! Obviously someone's mixed up the fact that she arrived by plane today. I thought you'd know her whereabouts, if anyone did.'

Louise looked at the letter she was still holding and clicked her tongue softly, which only served to increase Tony's frustration.

'Lou! Is something wrong? With Sam. . .?'

The urgency in his voice was not lost on Louise, who nodded to herself with a degree of satisfaction. But, just to make sure she wasn't mistaken, she said, 'Sam's OK. But tell me, Tony, how was Bangkok?'

Tony's voice softened. 'Bangkok was. . . beautiful. . .just beautiful.'

That was all Louise needed. Quietly she slid open a drawer in the desk beside her and slipped Sam's note to Tony into it. Not knowing what Sam had said in the note, she couldn't risk giving it to him. It might be quite harmless, of course. But then again, it might not.

Now, what to say to Tony that would have the desired effect? She decided that, for her purposes, the truth would do as well as anything. When he demanded again to know where Sam was, she told him, hesitantly, as though reluctant to break bad news to him, 'I. . .think the rumours you heard about Sam catching a plane were probably correct.'

'But that's ridiculous! Why. . .? Where. . .? It's not possible. She would have said. . .'

Louise quietly closed the drawer beside her. 'She obviously left in a hurry. Perhaps she did try to contact you,' she said.

'She could have—I've been tied up with Charles. Do you know anything about this, Louise? Don't hold out on me if you do. I must know. . .'

'Yes, I think you should know.' Louise spoke decisively now. 'While you were in Bangkok there was a call for Sam. It was put through to me in her absence. I was to give her a message. I left a note for her—I haven't seen her since she got back, so I can only really guess what her reaction was to the message.'

'Louise!' Tony's voice was threatening. 'If you don't stop beating about the bush and tell me what this is all about. . .!'

'OK, *OK*! The call was from someone called Michael. He talked as though he had some claim on Sam and demanded that she get in touch with him right away. He was in Adelaide, and I'm pretty sure she must have gone back there to see him.'

There was something like a groan on the other end of the line, and then a long silence, which Louise broke by adding, 'He sounded English.'

'He would!' The exclamation came over the line as though it had been emitted through gritted teeth. Then Tony said, with a note almost of despair, 'Lou, where do I go from here?'

It was a rhetorical question, but Louise's response was immediate and positive.

'To Adelaide.'

'To—Adelaide? You really think. . .?'

'It all depends, of course. . .'

'On what?'

'On how badly you want to. . .see Sam.'

'Very badly.'

'Then. . .'

'Of course, you're right. And, Lou—thanks!'

'Any time!'

Tony, about to hang up, had an afterthought. 'I don't suppose you know where I can find her?'

Louise, thinking she might as well add breach of confidence to the list of her other sins, said, 'I have the phone number he—Michael—gave me to give Sam.'

'That'll have to do, then. Fire away.'

Louise read off the number from the pad near her phone and, after another fervent, 'Thanks, mate,' Tony hung up.

The things I do for my friends! thought Louise, as she stripped off her uniform, donned a gown and went along to the showers. It's up to them now, she told herself. I just hope that between the pair of them they don't manage to blow all the good work I've done!

Tony drove home to East Winds in a fervour of impatience. There was no plane to Adelaide until tomorrow afternoon—on the same schedule as the one Samantha must have caught today. He could, of course, drive around, but it was a long journey, up to the top of the Gulf and down the other side, and he wouldn't gain much by doing it.

Arrived home, he took the slip of paper with the number Louise had given him from his pocket and studied it. He could try to reach Sam there. He even walked across the room and picked up the phone, then put it down again. If only he weren't so much in the dark about Sam's past. Knowing as little as he did, he could well do more harm than good by galumphing in blindfold, as it were.

He poured himself a drink, sat down and thought back over the last few days. Could he have been mistaken about what he felt had developed between himself and Sam during that time? After all, nothing definite had been said. He'd been too conscious of his impending divorce—had decided he should wait until his first marriage was over and done with and he could approach Sam with a clean slate. So, they'd laughed and talked and enjoyed themselves and exchanged a few light kisses in the moonlight.

And, after all that, she'd returned home to find some guy from her past demanding to see her, and had gone off without a word, as though nothing else in the world mattered. While he, Tony, had been occupied with Charles's patient this afternoon, with Bangkok like a lovely backdrop somewhere in his subconscious mind, Sam had already been on her way back to Adelaide to see this Michael person.

And a right fool he, Tony, would look if he mounted his white charger and took off after her, when she'd probably already forgotten he existed.

It was a good thing he'd sat down and thought this thing through.

Oh, he'd still go to Adelaide. But he'd be very circumspect in his approach to Samantha—ascertain the lie of the land first. . .which meant finding out just what this Michael meant to her.

He'd need to concoct some other reason for being in town, of course, something to fall back on if he discovered. . .what he hoped, quite desperately, he wouldn't discover.

He twirled his glass and pondered what that excuse would be. Then his brow cleared. Of course! Joe Stephens, his lawyer, had been asking him to come across for a consultation. If he hadn't had Samantha with him he would have stopped off on his way back to Wirrando and seen Joe then. And, also, there were two or three things he wanted to discuss with Trish. Joe wouldn't approve of his meeting Trish, but he didn't have to know.

Well satisfied with the results of his cogitations, Tony took himself to bed and slept soundly.

He had a busy morning next day—too busy to allow him to rethink his planned trip to Adelaide and possibly change his mind. Charles's ARDS patient had stabilised and Charles was happy to stand in for Tony for another twenty-four hours.

Three o'clock saw him boarding his plane, with a return ticket for next day in his wallet.

As he had anticipated, it wasn't easy to find a room in Adelaide during the Festival of Arts, but he was eventually successful in getting a cancellation at the Hyatt.

The Hyatt being within walking distance of the Festival Theatre, its foyer was thronged with patrons of the arts from all over the world. It was almost impossible, Tony found, not to respond to the hyped-up atmosphere. His reaction, he realised with interest, was to begin to feel much more positive about the favourable outcome of his own mission to Adelaide.

He went to his room, rang room service for coffee and, while waiting for it to arrive, unpacked his bag, wondering meantime how to set about finding Samantha. His only clue to her whereabouts lay in the phone number Louise had given him. Well, he would start with that.

He took the slip of paper from his pocket, poured himself a cup of strong black coffee and, sitting in the chair beside the telephone, dialled the number. A female voice answered, 'Earl of Zetland Hotel.'

So far, so good. The Earl of Zetland, he knew, was a small hotel in the heart of Adelaide. Had this Michael been staying at somewhere like the Hilton, he would have had Buckley's chance of tracking him down. As it was, he said, with all the charm he could muster, 'Good afternoon. This is Dr Tony Larsen speaking,'—good thought, that doctor bit—much more likely to get him the co-operation he needed. When he heard a kind of purr on the other end of the line he knew he'd not been wrong!

'I wonder whether you could help me,' he continued.
'A young man I need to get in touch with is staying at
your hotel. Unfortunately, I can't give you his surname,
but his Christian name is Michael and he's English. . .'

'Would you hold the line, Doctor? I'll see what I can
do.'

Tony waited. In a few moments the receptionist was
back. 'As soon as you said your friend was English, I
thought of the band, the one performing in the Festival
Fringe. Would that be right?'

Tony made a non-committal sound and the woman
went on, undeterred. 'Michael Platt. He's in room 112.
Would you like me to put you through?'

'No, don't bother, I'm not far away. I'll call round
later and see Mike.' Then, as the voice began to ask him
to repeat his name so that a message could be passed on,
he cut in with, 'Thank you so much for your assistance,'
and hung up, well satisfied with the results of his
sleuthing.

So! Michael Platt. And he was playing in a band in
the Festival Fringe programme. The Festival Fringe
image was avant-garde, energetic, bright. Tony had no
difficulty at all visualising Samantha in that scene.

His spirits dropped several degrees. Maybe he should
give up without going any further, but he quickly
rejected that idea. He was not at all sure what he was
going to do, but whatever it was he didn't have time to
sit here and ruminate. He must run this Michael Platt
to earth, that seemed to be the obvious first step.

It was already five-thirty and he'd be lucky if the
members of the band hadn't already taken themselves
off for a rehearsal, or a meal somewhere.

Tony put on his jacket and set out to make his way to
the Earl of Zetland Hotel, which was within easy walking
distance of the Hyatt. He had no idea what he would

say if he met up with Michael Platt. He'd just have to play it by ear when the time came.

In the hotel's reception area he passed by the receptionist with a brief nod and mounted the stairs to the first floor. Number twelve was not hard to find, and he was hesitating with his hand raised to knock on the door when a voice spoke behind him.

'Can I help you, pal?'

Tony turned, to see an extremely presentable young man, of medium height, with rather long blond hair, standing in the passage, eyeing him curiously.

'Michael?'

'Yes?' He didn't actually ask, 'Who are you?' but the question was there, and Tony was momentarily at a loss to know what to say. All he knew, suddenly, was that he didn't want to mention Samantha to this young chap with the alert, inquisitive blue eyes.

So he improvised quickly. 'I'm staying at a pub round the corner. Some guy said you could probably let me have a ticket to the concert tonight if I caught up with you.'

Michael's eye took in, in one quizzical glance, Tony's conventional dark suit, white shirt and subdued tie. He raised an expressive eyebrow and seemed about to say something disparaging, but apparently thought better of it. After all, he seemed to be thinking, if somebody wanted to fill a seat at the concert, who was he to discourage them?

'Come on in.' He put a key in the door and threw it open for Tony to enter. Tony did, and there, prominently displayed on the small table beside the bed, was a framed photograph of Michael and Samantha. They had their arms around each other, and were laughing, happy. . .young.

Instantly Tony felt as old as Methuselah—and terribly, terribly tired. What a fool he had been ever to think that Samantha could be interested in someone like himself!

He held out a hand for the ticket Michael had taken from a drawer and was presenting to him. When the ticket had changed hands, Tony recalled himself enough to reach for his wallet.

'That's all right, sir. It's on the house,' said Michael.

Tony winced at the 'sir'. But it reinforced how he was feeling about himself at the moment, and also the utter impossibility of Samantha ever coming to prefer him to someone like this young Adonis standing before him.

He said, 'Thanks a lot, mate. Be seeing you,' and departed, resisting the urge to break into a run, knowing he'd only be trying to run away from his image of himself—and he was stuck with that.

He had no desire to go back to his hotel—no desire to do anything, really. At length he dropped into a café he was passing and had some sort of meal. After that, he walked a few blocks, aimlessly, realising he had several hours to fill in before he could reasonably go back to his room and seek Nirvana in sleep.

The city was alive with traffic, pedestrians, lights and banners. Tony thought he had never felt so out of sync with his surroundings. He remembered those times he had been with Samantha when everything had seemed so right—so perfect, and felt a sudden urgent need to see her. Not necessarily to talk to her—just to see her and reassure himself that the magic of those days in Bangkok hadn't been wholly chimeric. He knew where she'd be tonight—at Michael's concert. He put his hand in his pocket and pulled out the ticket Michael had given him.

When he had asked for the ticket, he had had absolutely no intention of using it—it had just been the first thing that had come into his head to say. Now he was glad he had it. If he arrived at the concert late, after the lights had gone down, and slipped into a back seat, he could maybe catch a glimpse of Samantha when the concert ended, and decide then whether to speak to her or not.

The theatre complex where most of the Fringe performances were being staged was in the western end of the city. By the time he had walked there, the concert should be well under way. But it must have been late starting, because, when Tony arrived, the lights were still up. He slipped into a back seat, feeling even more, in his suit and tie, like a fish out of water.

And there, down near the stage, surrounded by a group of young things about her own age, and obviously completely at home with them, was Sam.

She was wearing the dress she had worn at the hospital barbecue, and it looked so completely right for the occasion that a suspicion crossed Tony's mind that she had bought it with this in mind. She was standing next to Michael, who had his arm about her waist, and she was laughing up at him, just as she had been in the photo on Michael's table.

Tony, all but hidden behind rows of people, was quite unable to take his eyes off her—until he saw Michael lower his head and kiss her lightly on the cheek, before disappearing backstage.

Tony had seen enough—more than enough. He waited only until the lights were dimmed, then made a hasty departure.

Samantha enjoyed the concert. She loved the music, revelled in the noise, the company, even in the adulatory looks Michael cast her way from time to time during the performance.

It was all great fun, and the knowledge that tomorrow she must face Michael and tell him why she had come to Adelaide didn't cast too long a shadow. Because beyond tomorrow lay a future she would hardly, yet, allow herself to dream about.

The members of the band and their friends went on for supper after the show. Sam joined in happily, smothering her slightly guilty feeling about Michael. After all, she had never been more than good friends with him. If their friends tended to regard her as Michael's girlfriend, that had been his doing, not hers.

Michael, however, when confronted by Sam in his room at eleven o'clock the next morning, saw things quite differently, and Sam's refusal to take his protestations of undying love too seriously didn't help at all.

'But you've *always* known how I've felt about you,' he insisted, looking hurt and bewildered.

'And *you've* always known how I've felt about *you*,' she reminded him.

'But I've come all this way. . .'

'To play in the concert,' she said firmly.

'Not only to play in the concert. I really thought— hoped—that after you'd been away for so long, you'd have. . .you know what they say, "absence makes the heart grow fonder".' He spread his hands in frustration.

'And I *am* fond of you, Michael. I've never pretended otherwise. But fondness isn't love.' Her voice softened on the last word, so that Michael turned and looked at her suspiciously.

'There's someone else,' he said accusingly.

'Not really—not yet, at least. But some day, yes, I hope. . .' She stopped, realising that Michael, wrapped in his own misery, wasn't listening.

'Michael, I'm sorry—really sorry! But there's nothing I can do to change things.'

'Will you be coming back to England?' he asked.

'I have no idea. As I said, there's nothing definite.'

He brightened. 'Then things could still work out for us.'

'No, I don't think so.'

'But you can't stop me hoping.'

'Just so long as you don't tell me, some time in the future, that I gave you any reason to hope.'

'Of course not.' But he sounded too cheerful, and, when Sam had said goodbye and left his room, she was unconvinced that he had accepted her decision. Well, time would take care of that.

Eleanor had arranged to leave the baby with a neighbour for a couple of hours and meet Sam in town for lunch at Pullman's, the Casino restaurant, if she could get bookings. Then she would drive Sam to the airport in time to board her plane.

Sam filled in the hour before meeting Eleanor at noon by browsing in shops in Rundle Mall. All she bought was a pair of earrings to go with the outfit she was wearing, which was a very smart two-piece slim-line suit she had purchased yesterday in a boutique Eleanor had taken her to on Unley Road.

Feeling light-hearted and free and attractive in her new gear, she wandered along to the plaza of the Festival Theatre for a while before going the short distance to the Casino.

Eleanor had been able to get bookings, and they went inside, chatting like old friends.

Not unexpectedly, there was a queue of people waiting to be shown to tables in the restaurant. As Sam stood in the foyer with Eleanor she found herself wondering what Tony was doing. Was he missing her—looking forward to her return? She was suddenly impatient to be on the plane again, heading back to Wirrando.

A waitress showed them to their table. It was on a slightly raised platform, beside windows that gave a magnificent view over lawns and gardens to what Eleanor told her was the River Torrens and, across the river, the spires of St Peter's Cathedral.

The restaurant was crowded, with tables being filled as quickly as they were vacated. Drinks waiters, waitresses and Keno girls flitted about.

Sam and Eleanor had a drink and then got up to help themselves from a magnificent smorgasbord. As they walked to the smorgasbord table, Sam caught a glimpse of a man seated several tables away with his back to her. Facing him, and talking animatedly to him, was an extremely attractive blonde-haired woman.

It wasn't altogether surprising, Sam thought, since Tony had been so much on her mind, that she should see a resemblance to him in the back view of the man at that table. Certainly he had the same dark, slightly wavy hair, the same tilt of the head as he listened to what the woman was saying.

As Sam began to help herself to an assortment of seafood from the smorgasbord, she wondered idly whether the man's face too would resemble Tony's. She looked in his direction again, just as he turned his head slightly, enabling her to see his face in profile.

It was—it had to be—it couldn't possibly be—Tony!

Her instinctive reaction was one of joy at just being in the same room with him. She almost started towards him, with some thought of asking what he was doing in Adelaide. He must have got the note she had left him and followed her.

Then the joy turned to bitterness. It was all too plain what he was doing here. As soon as Sam allowed her mind to control her emotions, she knew the identity of the woman with him.

It had to be his wife, Trish. Trish, with whom he was still in love, from whom he didn't want a divorce.

There was no doubt that they were deep in intimate

conversation. As Sam watched, Tony's hand reached out and took the woman's hand in his. Sam closed her eyes against the memory of the times he had taken her hand in just such a gesture. She had always told herself that charming small gestures like that came easily to him, but somewhere along the way she had allowed herself to be deceived into thinking that, with her, they meant something more.

They had meant precisely nothing. Her first thoughts about Tony had been the right ones. She hadn't a shadow of doubt in her mind that what was happening there, across the room, was the process of reconciliation she had always known he wanted.

Her heart felt like lead.

Eleanor, intent on loading her plate with salads and meat, was unaware of the change that had come over Sam. Sam moved along a little way to where a large square pillar hid her view of Tony and his wife, and wondered frantically whether she could make some excuse to Eleanor and leave.

But Eleanor had been so looking forward to this occasion, probably because, with a large young family, opportunities like this seldom came her way. Sam didn't want to spoil it for her—and anyway, what was to be gained by running away?

She became very absorbed in selecting her salads for another minute or so, then forced herself to smile and say to Eleanor, 'This is really something! I don't know when I've seen such a magnificent variety of salads.'

Eleanor looked as proud as if she had prepared them all herself, and they returned to their table in apparently the same frame of mind as they had left it some minutes ago.

CHAPTER ELEVEN

ALL the way to the airport, Sam agonised over whether she would be wiser not to return to Wirrando but simply stay in Adelaide until she could get a seat on a plane returning to London.

But the drive to the airport only took fifteen minutes, and as Eleanor parked the car and they walked into the domestic terminal Sam was still undecided.

And there, for the second time that afternoon, she saw Tony.

He was facing her this time, having just turned away from the counter, and was examining the ticket he held in his hand.

Sam just had time to register, before he raised his head and saw her, that he was looking extremely unhappy. Perhaps, after all, things had not gone as well with Trish as she had imagined from seeing them together. Or, and this was much more likely, he was miserable at having had to leave her again so soon.

Tony raised his head, saw Sam, and thought how different she looked from the relaxed, happy girl who had returned from Bangkok with him—was it only two days ago? The only thing of any moment that had happened to her since then was the meeting with her boyfriend. She had certainly looked happy enough when he had seen her with Michael, so the only explanation for the change had to be that she was upset at parting from Michael. Tony wondered why the guy hadn't at least accompanied her to the airport, but perhaps he had other commitments, rehearsals and things.

Eleanor too saw Tony, and, with a glad exclamation,

started towards him with her hand outstretched. Tony
and Sam had no option but to move too, slowly and
reluctantly, towards each other. Each was thinking it
was a good thing Eleanor was there, because, without
her, they would just not have known what to say to each
other. It had simply not occurred to either of them that
they might be returning to Wirrando on the same flight.

Eleanor noticed nothing amiss, but a few minutes
later, when it came time to say goodbye and she took
Sam's hands in hers, she exclaimed, 'My dear, your
hands are frozen! Are you all right? Not getting a
recurrence of the flu?'

Sam laughed, and tried to make it sound natural. 'No,
of course not. It's just that I'm always a little nervous
about flying when it comes time to board.'

Tony looked at her sharply, but she carefully avoided
meeting his eye, knowing he was thinking that she had
shown no signs of being nervous at any time during their
flights to and from Bangkok. She continued hurriedly,
'Thank you so much, Eleanor, for putting me up at such
short notice. It's been lovely.'

Eleanor replied, 'It's been great to see you looking so
well—so much more relaxed and happy than you were
when we were both in hospital after the accident. Make
sure you keep well from now on. I know how keen you
are to get back to England.'

Eleanor must have remembered her saying that in
Wirrando, thought Sam, because she had certainly said
nothing of the kind in the last two days. But, because
her return to London was now inevitable, she nodded
and said, 'Yes, there's no place like home, is there?'

Tony intervened stiffly, 'That was our second boarding call—I think we should go. Goodbye, Eleanor. Good
to see you again. Look after yourself and that infant of
yours.' With that, he turned and walked towards the

departure gate, and Sam had no option but to follow along mutely behind.

It was the same on the plane. Tony's seat was two rows in front of hers and the seat beside him was empty. It would have been the simplest thing in the world to tell the stewardess that they would like to sit together. But Tony didn't suggest it, and Sam was not about to, being convinced that he wanted to be left alone to think about Trish. All sorts of things would have arisen as a result of their meeting—problems to be sorted out, momentous readjustments to their lifestyle initiated.

So, though he appeared to be absorbed in the journal he had open on his knees, Sam was not deceived as, for the second time that day, she sat looking at the back of his head and feeling utterly miserable. Why, oh, why hadn't she stayed in Adelaide and caught the first plane home to England?

Tony, staring with unseeing eyes at his magazine, was wondering that very same thing. Why was Sam going back to Wirrando? She had obviously discussed her future hopes and plans with Eleanor and left her in no doubt that she wanted to go home to England. And, having seen her with Michael, he could understand that.

After giving the matter serious thought, Tony decided that Sam's strong sense of duty had prevailed against her own desires. Having committed herself to stay at the hospital for three months, she was determined to see it out.

Well, all he could do about that situation was to suggest to Matron when they got back that she release Sam from her commitment to the hospital. Yes, he would do that. After all, it was her happiness that mattered most.

Then there was his research project. At the present moment he didn't give a damn about that, but, for reasons of his own, he had made a big song and dance to Sam about how important it was to him. She was probably feeling bound to return and help him finish it, maybe even feeling—though heaven forbid!—that she owed him that much after the Bangkok trip. Well, that he *could* take care of himself.

Turning around, he realised for the first time that the seat beside Sam was vacant. She was gazing pensively out of the window and seemed not to notice him as he stood up and moved back up the aisle. When he came opposite her, he forced himself to smile and sound cheerful as he said, 'Hello there again. Mind if I join you?' His bogus geniality sounded completely unconvincing in his own ears. He wondered what she was making of it.

Her smile was wavering, altogether pathetic, as she said, 'Not at all,' and added, 'I was surprised to see you in Adelaide.'

For a fleeting second he wondered whether he should tell her just why he had been there. But she was finding life difficult enough already. He couldn't lay that on her as well. So he just said shortly, 'I had business to attend to there.'

'Oh?'

He must have heard the question in her voice, but he chose to ignore it, and Sam sat there wondering miserably whether to tell him that she had seen him with a woman whom she had assumed to be his wife. But she couldn't trust herself to mention it without becoming emotional, and the last thing she wanted was to reveal how seeing him with his wife had affected her.

After a brief silence, during which it was obvious that neither of them was deriving a great deal of pleasure from their thoughts, Tony said, 'I hope you won't misconstrue what I'm about to say. . .'

Wondering what was coming, she turned and looked at him with her clear, direct gaze, which more than once in the past he had found disconcerting, as he did now. After a lengthy, uncomfortable pause, the words came in a rush.

'I want you to know that, as far as my project is concerned, you're not to consider yourself bound to stay on in Wirrando.'

Sam knew at once what lay behind that statement, and why he had been so diffident about delivering it. Her presence in Wirrando would be an embarrassment to him, if. . .when his wife came back.

Since nothing whatever had happened between them which could possibly be construed as an affair, Sam couldn't quite see why that should be so. Unless Trish had learned—Tony might even have told her himself— that Sam had accompanied him to Bangkok, and Trish was making waves about it; maybe had gone as far as to issue an ultimatum that Sam should be sent packing or else. . .

But, much as Sam was already wishing she was anywhere but here, she didn't feel inclined to go slinking off as though she were indeed a guilty party.

'I have a duty to Matron. . .' she began.

'I thought you'd feel that.'

'The best I can do is speak to her and see how her staff replacement programme is going. If it's possible for me to cut short my time in Wirrando, I'll do so. I don't think I can promise more than that.'

Tony thought vaguely that her wording was a little strange, as though she were doing it to oblige him, and not because it was what she herself wanted. But just then the 'Fasten Seat Belts' sign came on and, as the plane began to lose height, he lost his train of thought in wondering whether Sam was nervous about landing as well as about taking off. If she *was* nervous, he thought, glancing at her, she was certainly concealing it well, as she had done on the Bangkok trip.

On the ground, he could do no less than offer her a lift into town in his car, which he had left overnight in the car park. She accepted, but said very little on the way, and when he dropped her at the door of the home, the atmosphere between them was, in a word, frigid.

Sam saw Matron that same evening, and told her she was anxious to return to England as soon as she could be released from her duties.

Matron looked at the girl hard for a moment, taking in the pale cheeks, the determined but unconvincing smile, and refrained from asking the reason for her change of mind about staying on.

Matron had her own thoughts about that—as she had had about the wisdom of Tony Larsen taking Samantha to Bangkok with him for several days. In these enlightened times, of course, nobody thought twice about anything like that, but all the same, with an attractive man like Tony and a lovely girl like Samantha, proximity had its own way of complicating situations. And Tony didn't really need any more complications than he already had in his life.

So Matron told Sam she wouldn't press her to stay against her wishes, although she would appreciate it if she would remain for another two weeks, at which time two of her nurses who were on holiday would be back, and there were hopeful prospects of at least one permanent addition to the staff shortly thereafter.

'I know you'll want to spend as much time as you can on Dr Larsen's project while you do remain, so I'll try only to call on you when it's really necessary,' she said.

That was the nearest Matron got to asking about the state of affairs between the doctor and her temporary member of staff, but Samantha's reaction was enlightening.

She hesitated, obviously unsure how to respond.

Matron observed that she had become even paler and that there was an empty look in her eyes. Matron's heart went out to her, but she kept her thoughts to herself and allowed Samantha to answer, which she did quite steadily. 'I don't expect to be doing anything more in that regard, Matron, so please feel free to call me as often as you need me. It will help to fill in the time until I go.'

'That being so, I shall ask you to take over Women's Medical as from tomorrow, for a week. Louise has worked a lot of overtime recently and I'd like to give her some time off before you go, in case our hoped-for extra staff doesn't eventuate. Do you feel well enough to work full-time yet? You still look a little washed out.'

'I'm quite well, really,' Sam assured her.

'Then you can start at seven in the morning.'

'Thank you, Matron.'

Sam went to her room to unpack and make sure she had a uniform ready for the morning. She knew that if she went to the dining-room for tea she would have to face a barrage of questions about her trip to Bangkok, so she made some coffee and toast in the pantry while nobody was around, then went back to her room and closed the door.

But Louise was not so easily deterred. She rushed in after she had been to tea, eager to hear about everything, but, as she only had ten minutes before she had to be back on duty and was in any case full of plans for her forthcoming, unexpected leave, Sam didn't find it too difficult to satisfy her with vague, non-committal answers.

Louise did think that Sam wasn't looking particularly happy—certainly not like a girl in the first flush of young love—and wondered, somewhat guiltily, whether her own intervention had gone awry, so she refrained from asking Sam about her trip to Adelaide. She didn't mention the note Sam had left for Tony either, reassuring herself philosophically that she had done her best for both of them and the sensible thing to do, now, would be to dispose of the note, which still lay tucked away in her drawer, before she went on days off.

At such short notice, Louise told Sam, she couldn't make elaborate plans for her break, but she had friends in Port Lincoln and would happily spend the time swimming or lying in the sun, doing absolutely nothing.

Sam wondered, after Louise had said goodbye and gone, whether she herself had ever been so young and carefree.

But, regardless of how she felt, she must put on a happy face for the next two weeks and never, never let Tony see how she was really feeling, in case he asked questions that she wasn't prepared to answer.

It required a Herculean effort to get herself out of bed next morning and on duty by seven o'clock. She made it with a minute to spare and promising herself a cup of coffee at the earliest opportunity. But she was not to be so lucky.

A girl of sixteen, who had attempted suicide by slashing her wrists, had been admitted in the early hours of the morning. Her name was Burdett Sanders, and although she had grown up and gone to school in town, nobody seemed to know a lot about her, least of all why she had done what she had done.

She was on a blood transfusion and would need constant supervision. She was, of course, Tony's patient, and Sam didn't need Night Sister to tell her that Tony had had a busy night. Even so, he had said he was to be called at once if he was needed, and would be popping in to see the patient at frequent intervals during the day.

When Night Sister had finished handing over and departed, Sam told the two nurses who were on duty with her that she would special the new patient while they went about their routine tasks, of which there were plenty at that hour.

Burdett, though conscious, was pale and unresponsive, and merely turned her head away every time Sam spoke to her.

Before too long, Sam realised, somebody was going to have to try to get the girl to talk. In a large hospital, there would have been an army of social workers to call on to help, but here, Sam suspected, with a sinking heart, the job would probably fall to her. Before that happened she must try to find out more of Burdett's background, of her family, her friends, her personality.

She was a pretty girl, with light brown hair, cut in the latest style and highlighted. Her skin was unblemished and her hands and nails well cared for. The toilet bag on the locker beside her bed was clean and of good quality, and the two nightgowns in her locker, though a little too brightly coloured for Sam's taste, were by no means cheap and nasty. Whatever Burdett's problem, she clearly had a caring and reasonably well-to-do family.

Sam had become so engrossed in doing what she had to do for Burdett, and wondering about her, that she did not hear Tony enter the room, of which Burdett was the sole occupant. It was only when he said, 'How is she, Sister?' that she became aware that he had been standing behind her for some moments.

If he had been surprised to see her there, he had had time to conceal the fact, and his manner was completely impersonal as he looked at Burdett's case-notes and asked Sam a question or two. She forced herself to smile and behave as normally as possible as long as he stayed.

But when he had gone, she was conscious of a slow burn of anger. He was behaving as though *she*, Sam, had done something to antagonise *him*, whereas the opposite was true. *He* was the one who had changed since their return from Bangkok, and he had given her not a single word of explanation as to what lay behind that change.

It was only by chance that she knew anything at all about recent developments in his life, and he must never know how disappointed and hurt she felt. That would be to reveal to him that she had begun to feel something more for him than just the friendship he felt for her.

She would concentrate all her energies on her work. A part of her duty, of course, would be to talk to Tony, as the one most likely to know what lay behind Burdett's attempt on her own life.

Her opportunity to do that came early in the afternoon, when Tony appeared again. He looked at the record of Burdett's vital signs and asked Sam one or two questions. As he turned to go, she said, 'May I talk to you for a few minutes, please?' When he hesitated, she added quickly, 'It's nothing personal,' and glanced significantly at Burdett, who was lying with her eyes closed, apparently asleep. But one could never be sure, so one never discussed a patient's condition within earshot of the patient.

She didn't know whether it was relief or disappointment she saw on Tony's face as he said, 'Of course.' Then he looked at her more closely, or, Sam thought, really looked at her for the first time that morning, and his tone softened as he added, 'You look tired. Can you take a break?'

'Yes. Nurse can relieve me for a while.' Sam rang the bell beside the bed and, when the nurse appeared, updated her on the rate of flow of the transfusion and told her to ring immediately if she had cause for concern about anything. Then she led the way out of the room and along the corridor to the duty-room. The other nurse on duty was there, charting temperatures, and responded immediately when Sam asked if she could rustle up two cups of coffee. Then she sat down, and Tony followed suit.

Sam came straight to the point. 'Somebody is going to have to talk to Burdett eventually,' she said.

'I agree.'

'Have I your permission to do so if the opportunity arises?'

He thought about that, then nodded slowly. 'I can't think of anyone I'd trust more to do it.'

Sam flushed at the compliment, but pressed on. 'That being so, I would like to know more about her—anything you can tell me that might be of help.'

'I've been thinking about that all day, and I've come up with—zilch. I've talked to her parents too, of course, and they're as mystified as I am, although they're still so upset they're probably not thinking very straight yet.'

At that point the nurse appeared, put two cups of coffee on the table and excused herself. Sam pushed one cup towards Tony and asked, 'What sort of people are they?'

'Ultra-respectable—to the point of being rigid, really. It's obvious Burdett has never been given a great deal of latitude to make her own friends, develop her own personality. . . She's an only child—not spoiled, but not deprived either, as far as material things go. As far as affection goes, I'm not so sure.'

'Are they patients of yours?'

'Yes—like almost everyone else in town. But they've never come to me with anything more life-threatening than colds and flu, and one doesn't get to know one's patients under those conditions, especially people like the Sanderses who don't really want to be known.'

'Hmm, that doesn't sound too hopeful. They haven't been in to see Burdett yet.'

'My orders—no visitors, even family, until tomorrow,

unless Burdett asks to see them, which I don't feel is very likely.'

'How soon should I—or anyone—try to get her to talk?'

'Don't rush it—feel your way. I'll be doing likewise, and I'll talk to Night Sister too, when I see her tonight.'

Involuntarily, Sam said, 'You must be tired!'

Tony looked at her keenly. 'And you. I'm surprised Matron shoved you back into things so promptly.'

'I asked her to.'

'I see. And. . .how long. . .?'

'Before I leave? I told Matron I'd stay for two weeks, for various reasons relating to staff problems.'

Again he said, 'I see,' then added diffidently, 'I hope you don't have any regrets about. . . Bangkok?'

'Why should I? I had a delightful time, thank you very much.' It was said prosaically, but Sam was thinking, If he knew how much I really mean that!

'I'm glad. I enjoyed it too.' His hand reached out as though to touch hers, but, remembering the scene she had witnessed in the Casino, she clasped both her hands firmly round her cup of coffee. He gave a tiny shrug and stood up. 'Well, that's that, then!'

'Yes.'

He looked as though he wanted to say more, but she intervened quickly. 'I must get back to Burdett. Thank you for telling me what you know about her.'

'Sorry it wasn't more helpful.'

She stood up and walked past him quickly, out of the room.

That encounter set the pattern for the next few days. When Sam saw Tony in the course of his rounds, they were punctiliously polite to one another. Each had reasons of their own for keeping up a pretence of cheerfulness when the other was around. Had they but known it, those reasons were remarkably similar.

Bangkok was not referred to again.

Neither they nor anyone else made any progress in getting Burdett to talk. She was resentful, withdrawn, patently unhappy. Her parents came often and sat with her, but Sam felt their seeming devotion was achieving nothing and almost wished they would stay away. Sam asked Burdett whether there was anyone else, any friends, she would like to see, but the suggestion met with such a strong negative response that Sam didn't pursue it, although she did feel that therein lay a clue to Burdett's emotional state, if she could only fathom it out.

Things remained pretty much at stalemate until the third day, when Burdett developed a fever and some jaundice, and a blood test revealed a lowered haemoglobin level. Sam had her own thoughts about the cause of those signs and symptoms, and could see by the gleam in Tony's eyes that he was thinking what she was thinking, and the blood tests he ordered confirmed that.

The results of the blood tests came back while she was on duty, and he called her into the duty-room. When she saw the forms in his hand, she raised her eyebrows and he replied immediately, 'Rh incompatibility.'

'Has she had a previous transfusion?' Sam asked.

'No. I asked her parents about that.'

'Then that means. . .?'

'Yes.'

'Phew! Do you think the parents know?'

'I haven't a clue, but we must talk to Burdett herself first. She's of an age to say whether or not she wants them told—whatever her story is.'

'Will you or I talk to her?'

'Both, I think.'

'You don't think she'll find that too threatening and clam up?'

'We can but try—and we can change our tactics if they don't seem to be working.'

Burdett was sitting up in bed, propped against pillows, and wearing a pretty pink nightdress. She looked at them with lowering suspicion as Tony pulled up a chair by the bed and Sam perched on the end of it.

Tony said lightly, 'Well, young lady, we've got your blood-test results back.'

A flush mounted Burdett's cheeks and she turned her head away, not looking at either of them. 'I don't want to know. You had no right to take them.'

Tony replied gently, 'We had to, honey. We want to do the best we can for you, if you'll let us.'

There was no reply forthcoming, so he went on, 'You see, when you started running a temperature, we suspected that you were having a reaction to the blood transfusion.'

Burdett looked startled at that, and asked quickly, 'I haven't got AIDS?'

'Absolutely not! We were testing for some incompatibility of your blood with the blood you received in the transfusion, and, because the reaction didn't occur immediately, we thought it could be what they call an Rh incompatibility. And that's what we've found.'

'Is it dangerous?' Again the response was immediate. At least, thought Sam, she's talking to us.

'Not at all, in normal circumstances. In fact, it's only likely to be a problem in someone who's been pregnant.'

Burdett flushed darkly, and tears came to her eyes. Sam reached out and took her hand, stroking it gently.

'What the test tells us, we think, Burdett, is that you've been pregnant at some time in the past—otherwise you wouldn't have had this reaction now. Is that right?'

'I don't know why you have to interfere,' said Burdett fiercely. 'It's my life, after all. I can do what I like with it!'

'Life's too precious to waste.' This was Tony again, and Sam wondered how she could ever have thought him lacking in sympathy. Her eyes, as they rested on him, would have been very revealing, had he been looking at Sam, but he was watching Burdett and was quite unaware.

'You've still got most of your life ahead of you,' he went on. 'It can be a good one. We really would like to talk about things and see how we can help you make it so.'

Tears were rolling down Burdett's cheeks now, and she was struggling against racking sobs. Then the flood-gates really broke. Sam continued to hold her hand, but they let her cry and talk, without interrupting, until it was all out.

It was a pathetic story they pieced together—of a child whose parents had expressed their love by trying to wrap her in cottonwool to protect her from life. Inevitably, she had rebelled and had become pregnant to a lad not much older than she. Her mother had hustled her off to the city for an abortion and nobody in Wirrando had any inkling of what had happened.

The restrictions when she returned home were worse than before. But she had managed to see the boy again and, more to spite her parents than anything, had resumed a sexual relationship.

She didn't tell her story in just those words, of course. When she seemed to have finished, Sam asked her softly, 'And are you pregnant again now?'

Burdett's eyes widened. 'I thought you knew that—from the tests.'

'No—we thought that was something you should tell us yourself, if you wanted to.'

When the girl said nothing, Sam went on, 'And that's why you tried to—take your life?'

Burdett shuddered. 'I. . .it was awful! I saw this programme on television about abortions—they said it was like murder. I couldn't. . .' Again the tears flowed, and this time Sam stood up and gathered the girl into her arms.

'And your parents don't know you're pregnant again, and you're frightened to tell them?'

'Yes,' chokingly.

'Do you want to keep your baby this time?'

'Oh, yes. But they'd never let me.'

'Don't be too sure. Parents can surprise you sometimes. Would you like Dr Larsen to talk to them and explain how you feel?'

'Would you?' Burdett looked up at Tony with a pathetic glimmer of hope in her red-rimmed eyes.

'On one condition—that you talk to them too, after I have—and tell them just how you feel about things like keeping your baby.'

'All right.'

Tony and Sam returned to the duty-room, where they turned to look at one another, simultaneously drawing deep breaths.

'Well done, Sam!'

'And you too.'

Suddenly the tensions of the past few days evaporated and they were back to how they had been in Bangkok—warm, friendly, peaceful.

Tony kicked the door closed behind them and took Sam in his arms. The only time that door was ever closed was if a sister or a doctor was making a private phone call, such as calling a relative of a patient with bad news. Sam knew nobody would walk in on them. She probably wouldn't have cared anyway. Without allowing herself to think, she returned his embrace, her arms going around his neck and her lips meeting and joyously responding to his kisses.

This was so right, she thought. Trish must be some sort of mirage that wasn't really capable of threatening this wonderful feeling she always had with Tony.

Tony was thinking that Michael Platt just couldn't be real—not when he and Sam could feel like this, so complete, so. . .right.

But Trish had loomed too large in Sam's thinking in recent days to be easily forgotten now. As Michael had in Tony's.

The magic went before the kiss ended. Their lips and their bodies still clung, as though endeavouring to reject what their minds were telling them. Sam wanted to cry out in rebellion, to tell Tony that he couldn't possibly belong to anyone else when they felt like this about one another. Her embrace tightened—she couldn't. . .wouldn't let him go. And, just for a moment, he held her more closely to him.

But the outcome was inevitable. Simultaneously their arms slackened and dropped and they drew back, looking at one another with sad, regretful eyes, and no words.

What was the use? Sam was thinking. Trish *was* real. It was her Tony loved and wanted. This moment with herself had been no more than a fleeting aberration, triggered by the emotionally-charged session with Burdett.

Tony was thinking, If only it had been possible! How could he ever let Sam go? But that was what she wanted, to go back to Michael who was young and bright, with a future Sam could share. Once she was with Michael she would forget this brief moment of. . .madness. She was so sensitive, so emotionally responsive to people's problems. . .she had been deeply touched by Burdett's situation. . .

Tony drew a deep sigh and murmured, 'If only. . .'

Sam knew what he meant. She nodded silently, while her heart echoed. . .if only. . .

He said, 'I must ring Burdett's parents.'

She replied, 'I'll leave you to it,' and went out, closing the door behind her.

CHAPTER TWELVE

BURDETT'S parents came to the ward the following morning and were closeted in the duty-room with Tony for more than half an hour. When Sam saw them leave, she went to the duty-room to see how Tony had fared with them, and found him sitting with his head in his hands, his elbows resting on the table. He looked up as she came in, and forced a smile.

'Was it heavy going?' she asked.

'Very. They finally saw the wisdom of letting Burdett keep the baby, but I'm not at all sure they won't leave town before her pregnancy becomes obvious.'

He sounded exhausted and despondent, and Sam wondered whether she should have a few words to say on the foolishness of a doctor becoming too involved with the problems of his patients. But all she said was, 'You did your best. People like that don't change their ideas overnight. Perhaps they'll adapt to the situation as time goes on.'

'One can only hope so, for Burdett's sake.'

'Can I make a suggestion?'

Tony shrugged and looked at her dully. 'Such as?'

'That you go home and spend the rest of the day tossing hay, or whatever it is farmers do at this time of year.'

This time his smile was spontaneous. 'Dr Hayes, I presume?'

'It doesn't take a doctor to see what would be good for you right now,' she said. Only someone who loves you, she added silently.

'You know, I might do just that—perhaps not toss

170

hay—I hardly know myself what's going on on the property at present.'

'If you do nothing else, you can talk to Bridie. I suspect she understands more than she lets on about everything.'

'I'm quite sure you're right.'

Tony stood up, hesitated, nodded goodbye to Sam, and went off, humming quietly to himself. She took the seat he had vacated, and gazed unseeingly at the wall for several minutes before, with a long sigh, taking her pen from her pocket and pulling the report book towards her.

Sam was due for days off, but she told Matron she would be just as happy to remain on duty and take a double break later, when Louise was back. Matron looked at her with the penetrating gaze she had been directing towards Sam every time their paths crossed lately, and asked, 'Are you quite sure? If you're feeling at all tired you should take your break now.'

'No, I'm enjoying being back at work.'

For two days Sam, working the p.m. shift, didn't see Tony at all. She knew he had been in early each morning, as was his habit, and she hoped he was taking her advice and spending at least some of his time out in the glorious sunshine they were having. She experienced a fierce longing to be there with him, enjoying the easy companionship they had had in Bangkok.

The influenza epidemic seemed to have burned itself out. All the nurses were back at work. Of their flu patients, one infant, who had had impaired lung function since birth, was still in hospital, as was an elderly man with a long history of emphysema. He was almost well enough to be discharged, but he lived alone, well out of town, and Tony was not taking any chances.

Beth was one of the few of the staff who had not had

the flu. But one night Sam awoke in the early hours to a subdued commotion in the home and, creeping out of bed and peering round her door, saw an obviously ill Beth, wrapped in a blanket, being transported along the passage in a wheelchair. It wasn't too difficult to guess what her problem was.

As Sam discovered when she went on duty next morning, Beth was down with more than just a simple bout of flu. She admitted to not having felt well for a couple of days, but she had said nothing, hoping her symptoms would disappear. Now the provisional diagnosis was viral pneumonia, and she was a very sick girl. Tony had been called out to see her at two o'clock in the morning, and Sam was with him now, just after eight, as he stood at Beth's bedside, looking serious.

Beth's breathing was laboured and she had a persistent dry cough which was obviously causing her pain. She was flushed and restless—delirious at times, complaining that everything ached, especially her head and legs.

Sam prepared Beth for Tony's examination and saw his face become even more serious as he auscultated and palpated her chest. Sam knew from the night sister's report that he had already ordered a chest X-ray and that would be taken as soon as the technician came on duty. Now he also ordered a Gram stain of a sputum specimen, and culture and sensitivity tests. Because Beth's condition was so similar to other cases they had had while the epidemic was at its height, he did not expect they would find disease-causing bacteria in the Gram stain, but a negative result would confirm that the pneumonia was of viral origin. Since culture and sensitivity tests could take several days, he ordered that Beth be started immediately on a course of amantadine.

She was also to be given low-flow oxygen, through a face mask as long as she was restless and in and out of

delirium. When she was more settled and able to co-
operate, they could change the mask for nasal cannulae,
with a flow rate not exceeding six litres a minute.

Beth might, in Louise's words, consider herself 'lowest
one on the totem pole', but it was evident in the next few
days that no one else shared that opinion. There was a
constant stream of enquiries about her condition, both
from outside the hospital and from members of the staff
popping into the ward to see how she was.

Her mother, as gentle and softly spoken as Beth
herself, was the only visitor allowed for some days, until
her condition had improved considerably. Then the first
one to be allowed in was the young man Sam had seen
with her at the barbecue at East Winds. Not many days
later Beth, sitting up, with shining eyes, was proudly
displaying a dainty engagement ring. No doctor's pre-
scription could have done more to speed her recovery.

Louise came back. Sam, puzzled, noticed almost at
once that Louise was acting oddly, almost as though she
was uncomfortable in Sam's presence. In the absence of
any other likely explanation, Sam put the change in her
behaviour down to her preoccupation with a new boyfriend she had met while she was away in Port Lincoln.
All the same, Sam was disappointed, and also slightly
envious of all the joy and gladness Beth's engagement
and Louise's new boyfriend were causing in the hospital.
She silently castigated herself for that, but, when she
saw Tony in the hospital, she found it difficult to be
other than remote and unbending towards him.

With Louise's inexplicable behaviour and Beth in
hospital, Sam could not face the idea of a four-day break.
When she heard that Matron had a new trained nurse
starting in a week's time and a nurse-aide not long after,
she went to Matron's office, and they agreed that she

should take a two-day break and then work for one more week before leaving.

'We have several mids due or overdue,' said Matron. 'May I roster you for duty in maternity for that week?'

'Of course.'

It was a busy week, but, since most of the expected mids were delivered at night-time, thanks to three nights of spectacular thunderstorms, Sam saw less of Tony than she might otherwise have done.

On her last afternoon, she was sitting on a low chair in the nursery, feeding a premature baby whose mother had gone home, when Tony appeared. He had done rounds that morning and Sam knew of no reason for him to have come back now. Unless it was to say goodbye?

He took a mask from the container by the door and put it on before advancing into the room. Masks were mandatory in the nursery—Sam herself was wearing one. Tony propped himself against a benchtop and stood looking down, apparently absorbed in the infant's feeding process.

'He's doing all right,' he observed. Since he and Sam had discussed the infant at length during morning rounds, Sam merely nodded, wishing he would say what he had come to say and go.

She looked up at him. He raised an eyebrow and she knew that behind the mask his lips were twisted in a self-mocking smile.

'I had a speech prepared for this occasion,' he said, 'and now I can't remember a word of it.'

'I'm relieved,' she replied lightly.

'Sounds as though you don't think much of my oratorical ability,' he said ruefully.

'On the contrary, I have the greatest respect for it.'

He looked blank for a moment, then said, 'Oh, yes, of course—Bangkok!'

Sam, wishing the subject of Bangkok hadn't arisen,

nodded shortly and concentrated all her attention on the baby. Nothing more was said as the child noisily finished the milk that remained in the bottle, then squawked in protest when Sam removed the teat from its mouth. She placed the bottle on the bench beside her and carefully raised the baby into a sitting position on her knee, massaging its back gently. It obliged with a satisfactory burp and Tony said, 'Well done, mate!'

That wasn't much of a handle on which to hang a conversation either, so Sam said nothing. The baby's eyes were heavy and she lowered it again, cradling it in her arms.

Tony said abruptly, 'I've come to say goodbye.'

'I know.' It was all Sam could think of to say.

He drummed his fingers on the benchtop, cleared his throat and said facetiously, 'Well, it's been nice knowing you.'

Sam's head jerked back as she looked up at him, a mute protest in her widened eyes.

'I'm sorry,' he said. 'Scrub that!'

That reminded her of his research project. She wished he would get it over with and go—this final confrontation was becoming more and more painful.

As if he had read her mind, he laid his hand on her shoulder, squeezed it quickly, said, 'Be happy, Sam,' and was gone.

By the time Sam had found her voice and said, 'You too, Tony,' he was out of earshot.

Sam had told no one at the hospital that she was not returning immediately to England when she left Wirrando. In fact, she had agreed to spend a month or two with the Purvis family, working as an *au pair* to enable Eleanor to fully regain her strength following the bus accident.

Sam felt very much at home with Eleanor and Eric

Purvis and the children. Timmy was eight, Belinda five and baby Jodi a five-month-old bundle of charms. Sam drove Timmy and Belinda to and from school each day in Eleanor's small car and relieved Eleanor of the care of the baby for several hours. Occasionally Eleanor allowed her to help with the cooking, but insisted that housework was not in Sam's contract.

In her spare time Sam explored Adelaide, the Mount Lofty Ranges and the mile upon mile of white sandy beaches. One day she and Eleanor strapped the baby's safety cot into the car and drove to Victor Harbour, Adelaide's retirement playground near where the Murray River joined the sea.

Sam lived a day at a time, avoiding any contemplation of the future, and gradually her restlessness subsided.

One warm Saturday, with Eric interstate for the weekend, Sam and Eleanor took the children to the beach. They erected a huge beach umbrella and sat beneath it, with Jodi asleep in her carry-cot and Timmy and Belinda splashing happily at the water's edge, within calling distance.

Unexpectedly, Eleanor said, 'Sam, don't feel you have to stay on with us if you'd rather be back home.'

Sam looked at her in surprise. 'But I wouldn't. . . Why. . .?'

Eleanor replied forthrightly, 'Anyone with eyes in their head can see that you're not happy. Is it Michael?'

Sam had mentioned Michael to Eleanor during her previous visit to Adelaide, calling him 'a friend from England'. Apparently Eleanor had added some embellishments of her own to that description of him.

Sam disillusioned her. 'Michael and I really were only friends, and we're not even that now.' Then, with a sudden surge of longing to at least speak Tony's name, she added, 'My problem isn't Michael, but Tony.'

'Tony?' Eleanor clearly had no idea who Tony might be.

'Tony Larsen.'

'*Doctor* Larsen?'

'Yes.'

'But I didn't know there was anything between you two.'

'There wasn't—I know that now. I let myself dream, but it was obviously all on my side.'

Sam went on to tell Eleanor about the trip to Bangkok and how nice Tony had been to her, even that he had kissed her. She said that Tony was married, currently in the throes of a divorce which, she was sure, he did not want. She told about seeing him with his wife in Adelaide.

'Did he see you?'

'No. It was while we were having lunch at the Casino that day.'

'I had no idea!'

Eleanor was silent for a few minutes, weighing it all up. At length she said, 'You know, Sam, I wish I could say differently, but I'm afraid I have to agree with you that you were mistaken in thinking he felt anything for you. I only saw you with him twice—at the hospital that day he brought you in to see me, and then at the airport, and I must say I didn't see anything at all that would make me think he thought about you—like that. In fact—and I wouldn't have mentioned this if you hadn't brought it up—I felt he was positively offhand towards you on both occasions, to the point of rudeness, actually. To be honest, I felt quite upset about it. I think you'd be letting yourself in for a big disappointment if you allowed yourself to go on hoping.'

Sam nodded miserably. Eleanor's clear-minded summing up of the situation made her realise, even more than she had before, the extent of her self-delusion.

'Sam, Sam! Come and see what we've found!'

Timmy was leaping about in great excitement at the water's edge. Feeling grateful for the interruption, Sam got to her feet and went to admire the tiny crustacean the children had found.

That night she reviewed her conversation with Eleanor and firmly resolved to put the past behind her and plan for the future. She was young, she had her career, and, as everybody always said, there were as many fish in the sea as ever came out of it.

But there wasn't even a crumb of comfort in the thought.

Eric returned from his weekend interstate, and that night Sam heard his voice and Eleanor's talking for quite a long time in their room across the hall from hers. Next morning Eleanor told Sam, over their morning coffee, when the older children were at school and the baby having her morning nap, that she and Eric felt they would not be doing the right thing by Sam if they kept her with them much longer. The best thing for her, they felt, was to return to England and get on with her life there.

Sam had to agree. It was very much in line with her own thoughts on the subject. At the same time, she realised it would not be easy to leave, because she had become very fond of the children in the last few weeks. It seemed to be the pattern of her life these days—to love and leave. In future she must be careful to avoid situations where that was likely to happen.

It was decided that she would stay with the family for one more week. She knew she should book her flight without delay. Several times she went so far as to look up the Qantas phone number, even to lift the receiver, but couldn't bring herself to make so definite a move towards severing her ties with Australia. If only she had news of Tony, she would feel happier about leaving.

On the second night after her conversation with Eleanor over coffee, as Eleanor and Eric were about to leave for an evening with friends, Sam mentioned that she would like to make an ISD call, if they did not mind.

'Of course not! Go ahead,' said Eleanor, who obviously thought Sam's call would be to her parents in England.

It wasn't England that Sam finally got through to, but Bangkok. Lena's voice sounded as clear as if she were in the next room.

'Sam—how lovely! Where are you? In England?'

'No, still in Australia. I'm leaving soon and just rang to find out about the baby. What did you have? Are you all well?'

'Didn't Tony tell you? A boy, Simon. Steve is over the moon, as you can imagine!'

'I'm so thrilled for you both. Congratulations. Actually, I haven't seen Tony for several weeks.' Sam explained briefly what she had been doing since leaving the hospital, then asked, 'How's Tony? Have you heard from him?'

'Yes, we did hear—that was why we thought you were back in England. We had a telegram a week or so ago, as well as a letter when he heard about the baby, earlier.'

'A telegram? Is he all right?'

There was a moment's hesitation before Lena replied, 'It's hard to say how he is. I've been wondering.'

'What did it say—the telegram?'

'Very little. Just "Divorce is final. Sam has gone".'

Sam's heart thumped heavily and for a moment breathing was difficult.

So Tony was divorced. She had been wrong to think it wouldn't happen. Had she been wrong, also, about his attitude towards his divorce? Was he feeling devastated now—or relieved? Lena was clearly as much in the dark about that as Sam herself.

And the rest of the message? 'Sam has gone'. Was there regret there—a lament, even? Or was she reading into it what she so much wanted to be there? In all probability, she told herself, it was no more than a statement of fact—informing Steve and Lena that Samantha Hayes, who had once been a guest in their home, had returned to England.

She had to know, and the clue to knowing lay, she saw with a flash of intuition, in Tony's past history. And only Lena could tell her that.

Her mouth was dry and her voice sounded strange to herself as she said, 'Lena, I want to ask you something.'

'If you want to stop over on your way home, we'd like nothing more.'

'No, it's not that, but thanks—I might take you up on it. Right now I need to know about Tony—about his past—about his divorce, his marriage.'

'You don't know?'

'Nothing.'

There was silence on the other end of the phone and Sam could almost hear Lena thinking. Eventually Lena said, 'I don't know. . .it's a long story. . .'

'Don't worry about the long-distance call. I have to know!'

'If Tony hasn't told you himself—I don't want to betray his confidence. . . Why do you want to know, Sam?'

In desperation, Sam blurted out, 'Because I love him!'

The long sigh that Lena gave came down the line and Sam, her senses acutely tuned, knew that she was both pleased and relieved.

'In that case, I'll risk Tony's wrath and fill you in on his past. Steve and I thought when you were here that, if something were to develop between you and Tony, it would be the very best thing that could happen to him.'

So Steve and Lena were on her side! That was promising. Some of Sam's tension left her and she listened as Lena talked.

'Trish and Tony married young, because both their parents wanted them to. I think they realised quite soon that they never should have. Tony was wrapped up in his work and all Trish wanted was a good time. Eventually they decided that it might help them solve their problems if they had a family.'

Sam gave a startled exclamation.

'And did they?'

'Yes—a little boy.'

'I had no idea. Is he living with Trish?'

'No. He died.'

'Oh, dear!' Sam's response was almost a groan. 'How. . .?'

'By then they'd moved to the country, in the back-blocks of New South Wales, partly to enable Tony to get off the treadmill and avoid going the same way as his father, who——'

'I know about that,' Sam interrupted.

Lena continued '. . .and partly to get Trish away from the bright lights and, I suspect, her drinking problem. But she hated living in the country and was restless and unhappy. Until Christopher came. She did seem more reconciled after that.'

'And?' prompted Sam.

'Christopher had a fall, when he was two years old. There was brain damage, and Tony, in the absence of another doctor, had to operate. Christopher didn't make it.'

Sam, appalled, was remembering the morning in OR

when Tony had had to operate on a little boy and had frozen up. Who could blame him?

Lena was continuing her story, talking quickly, apparently aware of what the call was costing Sam, in spite of Sam's assurances not to worry.

'Things went from bad to worse. Trish blamed Tony for everything—for the fact that they were buried in the country and weren't able to get what she called "proper help" for Christopher, and for Tony's failure to save his son. I have it on good authority that Christopher wouldn't have survived, regardless. But you can understand that Tony felt terribly guilty, even without Trish's accusations and recriminations, which went on and on. That was when they moved to Wirrando Bay. Tony refused to go back to the city and Trish refused to put in more than a token appearance every now and then at East Winds. And that was that. End of story.'

'How long. . .since Christopher. . .?'

'About two years.'

'Not long enough. . .'

'One would *never* get over it.'

'No.'

'We really hoped, when you were here. . . Tony seemed so much more relaxed, even happy. You say you love him, Sam. What are you going to do?'

'Find out whether he. . .loves me.'

'Atta girl! We'll be right with you. Let us know, won't you?'

'One way or the other. It's not cut and dried yet, you know.'

'No. But I have a feeling!'

CHAPTER THIRTEEN

Sam too had a feeling. In fact, she had a plethora of feelings as she said 'Goodbye,' and 'Thank you,' and 'I'll be in touch,' to Lena and hung up the receiver.

She endeavoured, without a great deal of success, to keep her feelings within bounds. That night, after dinner, she told Eleanor and Eric that she was going back to Wirrando for a short time. She gave no reason for doing so, knowing that Eleanor would try to discourage her. Eleanor did give her a long, penetrating look, but refrained from saying anything, other than to assure Sam that she was welcome at the Purvis home any time. She clearly expected Sam to come running back from Wirrando with a broken heart, and Sam knew she could be right.

She also knew she could never live with herself if she went home without finding out what Tony's feelings really were. He might, of course, greet her with casual politeness and ask what she was doing back in Wirrando. In that case, Sam decided, she would simply say that, instead of returning to England, she had been working for Eleanor Purvis as an *au pair*, and had returned to say goodbye to her friends at Wirrando before finally going home.

Feeling better for having a contingency plan in place, she decided to take a cab from the airport straight to East Winds. But sitting in it as trees and fields flashed by, she felt her self-confidence ebb. Her feet were like blocks of ice and there was a leaden sensation in her stomach. Or was it in her heart? She folded her arms across her chest and shivered slightly. The weather was

much cooler now than when she had been here previously and she was glad of the winter gear she had
bought in Adelaide. The designer pullover she was
wearing today with a blue skirt had cost the earth, but it
was worth it for the reassurance it gave her that she was
looking her best. She needed every bit of self-confidence
she could muster.

The cab-driver deposited her and her case on the
driveway at the front of Tony's house. She paid him,
and when he had driven away she stood looking at the
front door, willing herself to walk up and knock on it.

She needn't have worried. When she finally knocked,
there was no response. She waited a couple of minutes
and knocked again, with the same negative result.

It was an indication of her state of mind that the
possibility of Tony's not being at home had simply not
occurred to her. She realised now that he could be
anywhere, at the hospital, his consulting-rooms, or visiting a patient in some remote area. For all she knew, he
could be thousands of miles away, on leave, in Perth or
in Sydney. . .

It was not only her feet that were cold now. She was
cold right through. Leaving her case where it was, she
walked around to the rear of the house, her arms crossed
on her chest to stop herself shivering. On the back patio
a cushioned cane easy-chair was placed where it caught
the rays of the wintry afternoon sun.

Sam sank into the chair, closed her eyes and forced
herself to relax. Gradually her shivering ceased, and she
found herself wondering how long it was since Tony had
sat here, in this chair, and what he had been thinking
about then. Did he ever spare a thought for her, a
memory, perhaps, of their Bangkok interlude? Or had
he, since his divorce, immersed himself in his work and
his farming, to the exclusion of everything else?

She sat on, oblivious to the passing of time. Eventually, she knew, she would have to do something about her present situation. If she had been thinking coherently she would have ascertained whether Tony was home before letting the cab go. Her only option, now, was to go to a neighbour's and ask to use their phone.

She stood up and looked about her, wondering in which direction the nearest neighbour was to be found. For the first time she realised how different the country-side looked now, how green and fresh everything was. Of course, it would be. This was June, and therefore winter in Australia.

June! That rang a bell. She remembered Tony telling Gillian Marsh that Bridie's EDC—estimated date of confinement—was in June. Was Bridie still a lady in waiting, or had she had her big event? Sam felt she had to find out before she left. She walked across the lawn, then the grass, remembering the two earlier times she had done so with Tony, to the fence of Bridie's paddock.

Bridie was still there, some distance away, under the trees. And beside her was the most beautiful white foal. Sam called softly, 'Bridie, Bridie.' The horse raised its head curiously, and Sam repeated the call. Bridie, seeming to recognise the voice of a friend, began to move towards her, the foal following on long slender legs. Sam could have sworn there was a look of maternal pride in Bridie's eyes as she came to a halt on the other side of the fence.

Very slowly, so as not to startle the horse or the foal, she raised her hand and patted their necks, first Bridie's, then the foal's.

'You're beautiful, just beautiful,' she murmured to the foal.

'Her name is Sam,' a voice from behind her said.

Sam whirled round. Tony was standing a few feet away.

And it was there—everything she had hoped to see in

his eyes, as he gazed at her, and in his voice, as he said, again, 'Sam!'

He held out his arms and she ran into them.

Time stood still.

The sun emerged from behind a passing cloud and bathed them in light and gentle warmth.

For a long time words were superfluous, but the moment came when they wanted to hear it, and to say it. At first it was just endearments. He said, 'My darling!'

She said, 'Tony!' But she had never said it quite like that before.

He said, 'I love you.'

She said, 'I love you too.' And it might have been the first time in the world anyone had ever spoken those two words.

Then they explored the whys and wherefores.

Tony said, 'I've been thinking of you as back in England all this time.'

Sam smiled. 'I got as far as phoning Bangkok. Lena told me you were divorced.'

'And that's why you came back?'

She nodded, and he said, 'My darling!' again, then asked, 'But what about Michael?'

She was surprised by that. 'What *about* Michael?'

'I saw you together, in Adelaide, just after we came back from Bangkok.'

'I didn't know.'

'No. You looked so happy, so young. And I felt. . .old, and battered.'

She ignored that and said, 'I *was* happy, but not because of Michael. Because of Bangkok.'

Her eyes, those beautiful blue eyes, were saying everything he needed to know. He held her tightly for a long moment, until she murmured, 'I saw you too, that day in Adelaide.'

It was his turn to be surprised. He released her sufficiently that he could see her face.

'Where?'

'At the Casino. You were having lunch with someone I imagined was Trish.'

'It was. There were things about the divorce we had to finalise. But I didn't see you.'

'I took good care you didn't. I thought you and Trish were. . .reconciling.'

'Never!'

'I know that now, since talking to Lena.'

'And that was why you were. . .like you were. . .after Bangkok? Because of Trish?'

'Yes. And you were like you were because of Michael?'

'Yes.'

They gazed at each other, taking it in, before Tony reached for her again and held her close, so close that she could feel his heart beating against hers. 'It could have been. . .tragic. I could have lost you for ever,' he murmured against her hair.

Sam shivered and he held her even closer.

At length she said, 'Lena told me about Christopher, Tony.'

He said quietly, 'I'm glad. I would have told you, soon. I almost did once.'

She nodded. 'That night at the hotel.'

'I should have listened to my instincts when they told me you would understand.'

A little later, he asked, 'When did you first. . .er. . .feel some attraction. . .?'

He sounded so diffident she had to laugh. 'I think when I first opened my eyes and saw you standing by my bed, looking down at me. Of course, I hated you too.'

'I can't blame you.'

'When did you. . .?'

'Even before you opened your eyes.'

Suddenly he gave a great whoop of joy, caught her by the waist and swung her round, off her feet.

She was laughing breathlessly as she tried to regain her balance. 'What was that you were saying about being old?'

'Old? Never heard the word!' Then he added, with a note of wonder in his voice, 'Do you know, Sam, for the first time in years I don't feel. . .guilty.'

'I'm glad. Let's leave it like that.'

His heart was in his eyes as he said tenderly, 'I love you so much. Samantha Hayes, will you marry me?'

'With the greatest of pleasure.'

Bridie, with cocked head and bright eyes, watched the two humans on the other side of the fence for a minute or two longer. Then, as if deciding there was nothing more to be gained by staying in their vicinity, she whinnied softly and began to drift back across the paddock, her beautiful little foal called Sam close by her side.

4 MEDICAL ROMANCES
AND 2 FREE GIFTS
From Mills & Boon

Capture all the excitement, intrigue and emotion of the busy medical world by accepting four FREE Medical Romances, plus a FREE cuddly teddy and special mystery gift. Then if you choose, go on to enjoy 4 more exciting Medical Romances every month! Send the coupon below at once to:

> **MILLS & BOON READER SERVICE, FREEPOST**
> **PO BOX 236, CROYDON, SURREY CR9 9EL.**
> No stamp required

✂ — — — — — — — — — — — — — — — — — ✂

YES! Please rush me my 4 Free Medical Romances and 2 Free Gifts! Please also reserve me a Reader Service Subscription. If I decide to subscribe, I can look forward to receiving 4 Medical Romances every month for just £6.40, delivered direct to my door. Post and packing is free, and there's a free Mills & Boon Newsletter. If I choose not to subscribe I shall write to you within 10 days - I can keep the books and gifts whatever I decide. I can cancel or suspend my subscription at any time. I am over 18.

EP19D

Name (Mr/Mrs/Ms) _____

Address _____

_____

_____ Postcode _____

Signature _____

— MEDICAL 🖤 ROMANCE —

The books for your enjoyment this month are:

TENDER MAGIC Jenny Ashe
PROBLEM PAEDIATRICIAN Drusilla Douglas
AFFAIRS OF THE HEART Sarah Franklin
THE KEY TO DR LARSON Judith Hunte

♥ ♥ ♥ ♥ ♥

Treats in store!

Watch next month for the following absorbing stories:

CAUGHT IN THE CROSSFIRE Sara Burton
PRACTICE MAKES PERFECT Caroline Anderson
WINGS OF HEALING Marion Lennox
YESTERDAY'S MEMORY Patricia Robertson

Available from Boots, Martins, John Menzies, W.H. Smith, most supermarkets and other paperback stockists.

Also available from Mills and Boon Reader Service, P.O. Box 236, Thornton Road, Croydon, Surrey CR9 3RU.

Readers in South Africa — write to:
Book Services International Ltd, P.O. Box 41654, Craighall, Transvaal 2024.